AF434426

Compromised

Beyond the Law Book One

Eva Heart

Copyright © 2024 by Eva Heart

All rights reserved.

No part of this publication may be reproduced, distributed, or transmitted in any form or by any means, including photocopying, recording, or other electronic or mechanical methods, without the prior written permission of the publisher, except as permitted by U.S. copyright law. For permission requests, contact hello@evaheartbooks.com.

The story, all names, characters, and incidents portrayed in this production are fictitious. No identification with actual persons (living or deceased), places, buildings, and products is intended or should be inferred.

1st edition 2024

Contents

Chapter One

I can't shake the feeling that I'm being followed.

But that would be ridiculous. Why would anyone be following me?

I keep asking myself that, and so long as no good answer presents itself, I assume it's mere paranoia. A certain amount is expected. After all, it *is* my job to follow people. To spy on them, to delve into their inner workings.

So it's totally reasonable, I tell myself, to start imagining that I'm being followed. Seeing the same black car and too many stiff-looking men in dark sunglasses.

I spent the morning tailing my target through the aisles of a high-end supermarket while she bought four different kinds of yogurt, then brunch, followed by a brief stint at the gym. And now we've come to late afternoon, the frogs chirruping the end of the spring day from where they hide somewhere among the rows of manicured grass while I wait for her to go into her house. I find my eyes drifting down the street, searching for something, someone, watching me in turn.

I shake my head. I need to focus.

Josephine. That's her name. She's still in her gym gear: hot pink leggings and a cyan, low-cut bra that barely contains what it's supposed to.

I keep a small wardrobe in my trunk. Within it, an outfit for every situation. At the supermarket, it was a respectable-length, yellow summer dress. At the café, jeans and a light sweater as I watched over a latte from the back of the café.

I half expected my job to be done with then, given how many couples filled the café. But in the end, it was just another woman she met. They gossiped over scones, though I couldn't hear what about.

But Josephine's husband isn't interested in her dates with her girl-friends. That's not why he'd hired me. It was other men he was worried about. Craig is my regular kind of client. Rich and old, in varying measures. Married to someone typically less of both, but with more options and just starting to realise it. At least, that's what their hus-bands or wives are worried about, so they want me to investigate for them.

My work as a private investigator occasionally took other forms. Missing persons not taken seriously by the police, runaways, inher-itance claims. But this spouse following is the most common and the most predictable.

Josephine has been in the house for a handful of minutes. I watch the street for a car, or a man—anything aiming for her house while the husband is out.

I sigh. If no one presents himself, I'm going to have to go in. Craig gave me the key to their condo, which, he sourly noted, was paid for entirely by him. I think he expected me to snoop through her underwear drawer for love letters. But letters are outdated.

I don't, as a rule, like to sneak around someone's property, even given the go-ahead by *the one who pays for it*, but sometimes there's not really further recourse without it.

I liked it even less when I couldn't shake the feeling of being watched.

I look around one last time before I walk up to the front door. No cars, no suspicious lawn-waterers. Unless they are watching from one of the houses… *Stop it*, I tell myself. *You are* not *being watched. Now go do your job.*

Right. I need proof. I've been a private investigator long enough to know some people won't want to admit what they've known all along unless faced with literal pictures. So, in I go.

I let the door tap softly closed without latching behind me. The house is the kind of spotless only a live-in cleaner gets you. But there's no cleaner here right now. There *is* another visitor, though. I can hear the noises upstairs.

My shoes are soft on the shiny marble floors. Silent. I pass through the kitchen on my way to the stairs. There's a bicycle propped against the outer sliding door. He came in from the back then, and on a bicycle. A pair of mud-caked shoes have been discarded at the base of the stairs. Judging by the prints he left up to that point, I guess he's some kind of labourer.

I don't quite understand it, but the economic status of their spouses' lovers always ends up being a sore point for my clients. If the mister or mistress is not as well off, the wronged judges the standards. And if they're very well off, god forbid *more* than they themselves, they get competitive.

I step over the shoes and creep up the stairs. The bedroom door is open, the source of the telltale sounds pouring out. I don't go all the way up the stairs. I don't have to. I can just see their feet, tangled up, moving. The top of the stairs and the landing are littered with hastily discarded clothes, including hot-pink leggings.

I snap a quick video of the shoes and bicycle, being sure to catch the noises in the background. I don't video the couple. There are some lines you don't cross. It's surprising the amount of uses a disgruntled spouse can come up with for such content.

I slip back out the front door, down the street to my car. Still, I can't help but look behind me, but if I see anything, it's only shadows.

***

Craig is impatient. Not the type to wallow in blissful ignorance, he wants to know. So, I meet him the same day, in the closing hour of a small French café on the docks—the same place we first met when he hired me.

But Craig is also self-conscious. He glances around, as though checking that no one he knows sees him sitting here with me, paying to have his wife spied on.

"Relax," I tell him. "Else people will think you're the one having the affair."

That settles him a little at least. Then he looks me over instead. I ignore the glance at my chest and take the chance to rip off the band-aid. "I'm afraid you were right in your suspicions about your wife." Now he stops moving altogether. I sit forward. "She was with a man. He came to your house. I'm sorry."

Craig shakes his head. "God damn. I knew it." He takes a breath, rubs his eyes, then blinks at me. "Anything else?"

"Do you need to know anything else?" He doesn't answer, just stares at me, so I shrug. "He seems to be some kind of labourer. He showed up on a bicycle." I pull my phone out and show him the five-second video.

Craig snorts. But the humour doesn't last long. "I really thought she was different."

"It's up to you what you do with this information. Josephine is young. It could just be a mistake."

"This has been going on too long for that. Now I'll have to start over. I'm too old for this crap."

"Maybe try a woman closer to your own age," I suggest gently. Hey, what could it hurt to try dishing out some well-worn advice?

Craig looks at me like I've grown a second head. "Why?"

And here I was, starting to feel sorry for him. I reach into my handbag. "If you're happy to settle up now…"

"Ms. Burke?"

I look up at the intrusion.

Then keep looking up. The man standing next to our table isn't really a giant, but he does look like he could crumple the chairs, the table, and us just by resting his fist on the saltshaker.

Two more men are hanging out off to the side, trying not to look alert. Based on their stature, they may as well have just kept their uniforms on.

I sit back in my chair, addressing the big guy. "Officer?"

He frowns, and looks down at his plainclothes, as though checking he didn't put the wrong outfit on by mistake. His frown deepens.

"We'd like a word." I turn my head. This voice comes from someone of considerably less impressive stature. Dark, straight hair, glasses. Something tells me he writes the cheques. Despite that, he looks harmless enough. If I had to pick who to run from…

Craig's eyes have been wide since I said *officer*. He looks ready to bolt. When the dark-haired officer glances his way and adds, "You too, sir," the blood seems to drain out of his face.

Craig looks accusingly at me. "What have you gotten me into?!"

"Nothing," I tell him calmly, then look between the two framing our table. "He's just a client. Let's not complicate this."

A brief silence. A nod from the big guy. "You're free to go." And he does.

"I'll invoice you," I call after Craig.

I sigh as the officer takes Craig's seat, dwarfing it. Absently, I wonder if the flimsy wooden chair will hold him, but it's not really my problem. Whatever this giant and his friend wants, however, is.

"How did you get those?"

"What?"

The other man, the one with the glasses, pulls up a chair at my elbow. "The photos you were showing to your client. Don't deny it."

"It was a video. And I took it with a camera?"

"Did you have permission to be on the premises?"

"From the husband, yes. He had some well-founded doubts."

"Was this permission in writing? Signed?"

I narrow my eyes. I know this isn't really about some minor misdemeanour. You don't send the hulk in plainclothes to hand out parking fines. They've been watching me all day. They want something else. Or they have something else on me. I know how this is going to go. I could refuse to answer them, demand some kind of warrant or lawyer, but something tells me the result will be similar.

"It was more of a spoken thing."

"You were trespassing."

I sigh heavily. "We all know you want to bring me in. Let's not skip around it."

"Have it your way."

***

I wait for an hour under the single flickering light of the interrogation room. I'm not cuffed; I guess they don't quite have the grounds for that. I don't know exactly what they *do* have the grounds for, and that makes me nervous. I'm also not given anything, not a phone, not even a coffee.

When the first officer finally comes back in, he's in different clothes. Less polo-shirt and more button-down, but still struggling to contain his gigantic shoulders. He has a lanyard, and I catch his name. Agent T. Gertin.

"Is the 'T' for tiny?" I ask as he sits across from me.

"Theodore."

"Great. Listen." I sit up from where I've slumped. "I understand you're just doing your job..." Theo tilts his head a modicum at this. Like he's expecting a load of crap and just waiting to see what form it comes in. "But me and Bici," I say, naming the Bureau of International Criminal Investigation and the building I was brought to, "Sort of have an agreement. I stay out of your way, throw you the occasional lead, and you stay out of my business."

Theo doesn't look impressed. "I don't see any evidence of such an agreement."

"It was kind of unspoken."

"Hmph."

"Come on," I sigh, spreading my hands. "Don't you have better things to do than chase minor infringements? So what if I didn't have a signed form? I know how much you guys love your paperwork, but come on... I'm on your side!"

Before I've finished talking, he stands and tosses a sheaf of papers across the desk. I stare at the first page as it slides to a stop in front of me. "What's this?" I ask, hoping he didn't notice the delay

Theo leans his knuckles on the table. I gaze innocently up at him. He's fairly cute, if you're into the angry ones that look like they could rip you apart with a badly timed sneeze. "You know full well what it is."

"I do?" I ask. I need to buy time. How am I going to talk my way out of this one?

"This is your bank account."

"Hm, don't think so. I'm with the good ole' Trust City Bank."

"Mm-hm. This is your *other* bank account. The offshore one." When he takes the papers back, he pretends to flip through them, though I'm sure he must know everything that's on there already. "In Switzerland." He shoots me a side-long look. "*Very* creative of you."

My jaw tightens. "You're allowed to have more than one bank account."

"You are, if you're not using one of them to evade tax."

"Officer…" I try to keep a humorous lilt in my voice, like this is all just a big misunderstanding. I could try the flirtation route, but I sense I won't have much luck there. Either way, it turns out he's not buying it.

"You could go to prison for tax fraud, Ms. Burke."

"Jesus," I cringe. "Just call me Elsie, for pity's sake."

At that moment, the door opens. The second man, the one with glasses, walks in. He's in a muted but expensive-looking suit. There's a binder under his arm. Theo doesn't glance back. Rather, his focus stays on me. "We have the grounds to take it and throw you in prison."

I open my mouth to say what? I don't know, but the scratching of a pen on paper draws my attention to the end of the metal table, where Glasses is jotting something down.

"You couldn't have taken notes from the other side of the glass?"

He glances up, looking mildly surprised to have been addressed. "Ah, right. Ms. Burke. I'm Agent Melvin."

"Charmed, I'm sure." Then I shrug. "So why haven't you thrown me in prison yet? If you have everything you need? Why not arrest me for that instead of trespassing or whatnot?"

Melvin speaks up, putting down his clipboard and putting himself at eye level by taking the seat across from me. "We have another proposition for you."

I raise an eyebrow. Melvin glances up at Theo, who stiffens a little. "We'd like you to help us out," he says, like a man not used to saying anything remotely like that.

I snort. "Help *you*? What? Your wife been working late?"

His look has me shrinking a little. "I think you'll find you have little choice, *Elsie*."

"What my partner is trying to convey..." Melvin begins but stops when Theo slides a printed photo across.

I lean to see. A man, in some kind of lounge that's shrouded in shadow everywhere but where an orange-tinted light hangs above the booth he's in. There are two men, actually, but only one in focus, so I assume he's the one I'm meant to be looking at. He's sitting forward, elbows resting on his spread knees, a slight smirk on his lips. His hair is cropped short, and he has a slight shadow of a beard.

"Cute," I say, pushing the photo away a little. "Not really my type, though."

"No? Well, you're his type."

"Come again?"

Theo gestures vaguely at me, like I might be some kind of growth, which isn't really an answer, but he moves on anyway. "You're looking at Finn Damron."

"Well, that sounds made up."

"Be that as it may..." Melvin cuts in this time, evidently playing some kind of good-cop. "He specializes in fake identities. New names, jobs, a cover story, that kind of thing. All you need to know is he's a risk to national security."

I raise an eyebrow. "And why do I need to know anything about him? You want me to investigate him? Surely you have a lackey or three for that. I, for one, found their plainclothes *very* convincing."

Melvin ignores my jab. "It's not exactly your investigative skills we're after."

I frown. I'm pretty sure I don't like where this is going. "Were you just waiting for an excuse to bring me in and corner me with this?"

Theo shrugs. "Sooner or later, you were gonna do something at least mildly illegal."

"Thanks... You know, you could have just asked."

"Your history doesn't exactly show an altruistic streak. This is not something we could present to you and have you turn down, as then you would have information we can't afford to have spread around. Would you have agreed?" Melvin asks.

Resisting the urge to argue over the non-altruistic thing, since first I'd need to think of a good argument, I say, "Well, everything has a price."

"It's fortunate you think that way..."

The door opens. Both men stand. I opt not to. A man who looks like he needs to be hooked up to a coffee IV walks in.

"Sir," says Melvin, opening his hand towards me. "This is PI Elsie. This is Albert Brennan, head of Bici operations."

That makes sense. Not much time for sleep, exercise, or self-care, I guess. "Miss Burke."

"Yeah. That is me, still."

"We've been watching your operations for some time." I'll bet. "We thank you for your part in helping us."

"I don't know if I've agreed to anything yet…"

"Oh." Albert frowns, glancing at Melvin like he came in too early. "Well, I hope you'll find it in your heart. Seahorse is a dark organisation, and we'll all be safer without it."

I feel like he's reading promotional material to me. I raise an eyebrow.

"This is some recruitment," I say, glancing between them all.

Melvin clears his throat. "I'm sure she will, sir."

Gotta appreciate some misplaced optimism. Albert buys it, nods at me. "Well, you've got two of our best agents on the case. They'll take good care of you," he adds on his way out.

I stare at the closed door for a beat, then at Melvin as he sits back down. "Mind telling me what the hell this is all about? What's Seahorse?"

Theo answers instead. "We want you to ingratiate yourself to Mr. Damron." He taps on the photo again. "Get close to him and help us catch him."

I have the urge to burst out laughing. I contain it. "I have a lot of questions…"

"We've been watching him for a while now. We even brought him in once, but he managed to escape. Now, every time we're closing in, he manages to slip out of our grip. Like a fish."

"Eloquent."

When Theo sits down, I swear I hear the metal chair creaking. "We just need you to distract him. Get him somewhere we can corner him, then I make the arrest. It's that simple."

"Right." I fold my arms. "And I suppose this distraction would come in the means of…"

"Your charms," he says, with a certain amount of irony.

"Uh-huh." I narrow my eyes. "Why wrangle me in for this? Why not one of the lovely ladies pushing paper out there? I'm sure they'd be happy to take one for the cause."

Theo opens his mouth, but I'm almost relieved when Melvin takes over for this bit. "Because you bear a strong resemblance to the kind of women he's had in his life up to now, however briefly. He has a type. You're it."

"Flattering."

"Don't take it personally," Theo advises.

"Of course not. Why would I do that?" I sigh, then wriggle in my seat. My butt is going numb on this awful thing. "So, to sum up, I go seduce Mr. Security Risk so you can interrupt us mid-coitus to arrest the guy."

"That's the gist of it."

"And what if that's not my idea of a hot date?"

Melvin's smile becomes strained. Theo sits back, crossing his arms. He looks smug. "Well, Elsie, I suppose you can kiss your money good-bye."

Chapter Two

After a night of silently cursing Bici, its agents, and any children or pets they may ever have, I'm in the back of a surveillance van disguised as a delivery van.

The interior is almost exactly how it looks in the spy movies. Except the people inside are somewhat sweatier, and the air is hot and stifling. Added to this, the ride feels none too safe, the measly belt that goes around my hips seems ineffective—a hindrance even, given that each time we take a corner a bit too fast all I can wonder about is just how well bolted in the bulky machines that surround me really are.

It's a great distraction, expecting something the size of a fridge to come sliding at me any moment while Officer Theo—who seems unconcerned, probably because he very likely weighs more than a fridge—debriefs me.

"Finn is his real name. He's going by Patrick right now, after a lot of other iterations. We became aware of him when he started becoming significant in the stolen ID business. He's since moved up to actually manufacturing them, though we haven't been able to figure out where or with whom." Theo gives me a look like he knows I'm not listening closely enough. "This man is dangerous. We suspect him of helping some of the most dangerous people currently in the country to get across the border in the first place. And you don't play in those circles without rolling a few heads. So don't go off half-cocked."

"Could we possibly use a different turn of phrase for now?"

The truck comes sharply to a stop, as is its prerogative. Except this time, it stays there, the engine cutting off. I breathe a sigh of relief, although that isn't a very pleasant experience when it comes to the inhale.

I roll my shoulders inside my ruffled blouse, the pencil skirt pinching at my waist. This isn't my style at all, all the way down to the short, smart black heels with a little extra ankle showing, and the stockings underneath them. But the 'working woman looking for a little distraction from her regular life with a possibly dangerous man' is the look they've decided to go for.

The back door of the van slides open with a loud clang, letting in a gush of cool, refreshing air and also Melvin. He got to ride up front. Lucky him.

"We ready?" he asks, stepping up into the tray.

"Just about," Theo answers.

Melvin is untangling some kind of black wire. When he comes toward me with a mini microphone on the end of that wire, I put my hand out to keep him at a distance. He looks up surprised, as though he never expected that I wouldn't just let him root around inside my shirt. "What the hell is that?" I ask.

"A wire," he tells me. "Anything he says might…"

"Are you trying to get me fucking killed?" I snatch it out of his hands and toss it at Theo's chest, which is hard to miss. He doesn't bother to catch it, just watches it drop to the ground. "Just exactly where do you think I'm going to hide that thing, given the parameters of this little mission?"

Melvin sighs, scratching his head. Theo nods at him. "Alright. The earbuds instead," he instructs, then turns to me. "We'll only be able to hear what you're saying, rarely what anybody else is saying. Toss them before he gets too close to your ears."

I guess that's better. I take the small, clear devices and jam them none too comfortably into my ears.

"Can you hear me?" The tinny, and most importantly very loud, voice reverberates inside my head.

I jump and nearly rip the earbud right back out. "Jesus, you didn't say they did that! Turn it down!"

"Better?"

"I guess it'll do," I sigh.

"Got your phone?"

"Yes…" I say, slowly. Like hell am I going to let them take that too.

"Put both of our direct line numbers in there, too. Just in case."

That done, I roll my shoulders and slide my phone back into my little handbag. "If you know he's in there, why not just waltz in and arrest him now?"

Theo gives me a look that tells me I'll never understand. "He's not the only criminal to enjoy Belough Lounge. There's plenty of exits he'll know about that we don't, and plenty of friends too."

"Also, he'll know our guns are useless because we won't open fire inside the premises," Melvin adds.

"Sure. Whatever."

"You need to follow our instructions, Ms. Burke. This man is dangerous. Cunning. You cannot trust him." Theo gives me a hard look.

Something in his tone has me raising an eyebrow. "Something personal against this guy?"

His look, somehow, gets harder. I regret asking. "Do as I instruct, Ms. Burke."

I raise my hands. "I get it, okay? Can we get this over with before he wanders off with someone else for the night?"

"One more thing." Before I can turn to face Theo again, I feel something cold at the back of my neck, just under the hairline. Then a sharp, sudden pain makes me gasp and spin around. There's a small device in Theo's hand; whatever he just used. I tenderly touch the back of my neck, bringing a small spot of dampness—blood—away.

"The fuck was that?"

"DNA sample," Theo murmurs, sliding his weird little gun back into its box.

"In case... Well..." Melvin hesitates to explain, passing me a cotton pad.

I spread my hands, giving Theo my darkest look. "A saliva swab wouldn't do?"

Without meeting my eye, he tells me, "This is more thorough. Are you ready?"

I press the pad over the tender spot, wincing a little. I would like to yell at him a little more. You can't just *shoot* someone in the back of the neck. But I see he's too stubborn for me to get any kind of satisfaction out of it. Really, neither of these men seems to know how to interact with a woman.

I step down onto the tarmac. It's a little shiny from the recent shower, the streetlights glowing and dispersing orange across it.

When Melvin joins me, he points up over the low buildings surrounding the back-of-business alleyway we're in and up to a narrow silver skyscraper silhouetted against the dark, light-polluted sky. "There's your hotel. We got you a room on the east side. All set up for you." He's talking as though I'm getting a free holiday, but I doubt I'll get to enjoy the minibar.

"And there," Theo adds, pointing to a thicker, darker skyscraper, "is where we'll be watching from."

I squint up at the two buildings, then back at the parking lot and back of house bins of the lounge. "Got it, Peeping Tom."

Ignoring me, Theo hands me a white hotel room card. "Get Mr. Damron back there. Nowhere else. We'll do the rest."

"And if I can't?"

"Improvise." Then he's climbing back into the van.

Melvin leans out. "Stay safe, Ms. Burke!"

Then Theo slams down the roller door. I turn to the side alley leading to the front of the lounge. Is it too late to disappear into the night?

***

By the time I walk into the lounge, the bleeding at my hairline has stopped, and I toss the pad in the bin by the door. It itches, but I resist reaching to touch the spot.

I go straight up to the bar, which dominates the center of the room, and, as instructed, take a seat. Apparently, they thought I needed to be walked through the entire process of how to pick up a man.

I order a cocktail. Because hell, they're paying. When it comes, I hold it to my lips while I cast my eyes around the interior.

Semi-private booths line the walls, all with subtle, low-hanging orange lights above them. Further beyond the bar, the venue gets darker. I can hear music pumping from a dark archway on the far wall and see lights of changing colours. Theo was very adamant that I not go back there. Apparently, that was where the *really* dangerous ones hung out. Nonetheless, it is tempting...

Then I spot Finn. He's in one of the booths, a couple back from the ones nearest the bar. It's definitely him, though his hair has grown out a little, his beard too. He's wearing a black T-shirt. As I sip my drink, I need to appreciate that there's something about simple black t-shirts on already hot men that just multiplies the effect.

I pull my eyes away from him because Finn is not alone. With him is a man of considerably less allure. Twitchy and pale, his clothes are baggy in a way that accentuates a posture so terrible that he looks a little like a hunchback. I would never justify judging a book by its cover, but...

I shouldn't look for too long. I pivot back to face the bar, chafing in my corporate-sexy getup. Slightly unbuttoned blouse, tight pencil skirt, big hair. Like a woman who might already be having an affair and wouldn't mind adding another. Nothing like the idea of getting a high-strung woman to let loose, especially when she might have a witless husband waiting at home. I can attest to that well enough, given the majority of my clients.

"He's talking to Elmer Gage. A known drug trafficker in this area." Theo's voice comes tinny through my left ear. I hide a grimace with another sip of my drink. It's still too loud.

"A drug lord named *Elmer*? No wonder he wants a new name." Then I frown. "Hey, how the hell can you see what I see?"

Louder now, *"Don't speak out loud, Ms. Burke! Keep your comments to yourself."* A short pause. Long enough for me to look down at my blouse, squinting at the buttons. *"Yes, the camera is in a button. Now please act normal."*

Prick, I think, but refrain from mumbling it. I straighten my back and order another cocktail. I suppose it's waiting time.

***

As it turns out, I don't have to wait long. Which is fortunate because the cocktails here taste dangerously good.

Finn leaves his booth and his drug-lord friend. I watch him come up to the bar out of the corner of my eye, just around the curve from me. That's good. Out of touching distance, but within shouting distance.

"Remember, whatever you do, take him to the hotel room we assigned you. Do not go home with him. We cannot protect you there," Theo reminds me, again, as though to show he really means it. Or maybe he can just tell I'm not taking it seriously. I know as well as anyone the juiciest secrets are inside people's homes.

However... I also don't want to be on my own with a potential psychopath.

I call the bartender for another drink, to bring attention to myself. I feel it working, feel Finn's attention turn towards me and linger. Then his own drink arrives, and I make the first move.

I just look at him until he looks back at me.

So it's a simple move, but at least it's hard to misinterpret.

There's no double-take, no breaking of eye contact. He holds my gaze with a slight curve of his lips. No lack of confidence there, then. I sip my drink without looking away.

That appears to be enough of an invite. He picks up his short glass and closes the space between us until he's by the barstool one over from where I'm perched.

"I don't think I've seen you here before." His voice is deep, a little dry. There's a slight accent I can't yet place.

"That's because I've never been before." I smile.

"Careful, this part of town can be dangerous."

Of course, he thinks I have no idea of the types that really come out of this venue. I affect a laugh. "Really? I guess I might need protection then, huh?"

Leaning on the bar, he asks, "What brings you? Felt like blowing off steam?"

"Something like that." I glance over at the booth. Elmer's head is down. He looks sullen. "Am I keeping you from your friend?"

A short shake of his head. "Oh, we're all done."

"Lucky for me."

"It could be."

I smile, casting my gaze downwards, reverting to being just a little bit demure. Finn doesn't seem paranoid or suspicious right now, but if he's evaded the law so many times that they're trying this, I'm sure he's more than aware of their interest in him.

"I'm Finn."

I glance up, meet his smokey eyes. He's giving me his real name? That's a good sign... or a very bad one.

"Elsie," I say. I can *feel* Theo wanting to admonish me through the headset. I really need to get rid of the thing. Flush it down the toilet, dump it somewhere no one will find it until I'm long gone.

I was told to use the name Stephanie. But really, what's Finn going to do? Google me? Send my first name to some hacker friends of his? This should all be over before he has the time, anyway.

Drug-lord Elmer gets up and leaves. My eyes follow him. "He doesn't look too happy," I comment.

Finn glances over his shoulder, then turns back to the bar. "Just a business disagreement."

"Business, here?"

"You'd be surprised."

I wouldn't. But I act like I would be, anyway. This isn't about *my* pride, after all.

Finn is tilting his head at me. "You look like you work in one of these big skyscrapers around the place."

I smile. "Caught me! I worked late." Then I raise an eyebrow. "You don't look like you work in one of these big skyscrapers."

Finn huffs a laugh. "You could say I'm just passing through. Buy you a drink? You're running a little low."

"It's getting late…"

"Then I'll buy you half a drink." He sits.

I laugh. "I guess I'm convinced." I rotate on my stool, letting my stockinged knee brush the side of his hip 'accidentally' as I turn to face the bar. I glance sidelong at him. His hair is a lighter brown than the picture, as though sun-bleached. It softens his face a little. A handful of freckles make him look deceptively innocent, though meeting his eyes takes that effect away almost instantly. There's too much intelligence there.

He's someone I might have picked up, anyway. I remind myself that I'm not actually going to get to enjoy any sex with him. It might not even get to sex before they barge in and arrest him.

The bartender places my cocktail on the bar in front of me.

"Where's home?" I ask.

"Right now, in the city. You?"

"Right now, a room in the Rise," I say, naming a hotel. That should spell my intentions pretty clearly to him.

It does. He chuckles. "Oh yeah? That's not far."

I arch my back a little. "No, it's not."

When Finn faces me fully, his hand slides onto the top of my knee, resting there, hot and foreign and somewhat exciting. I'd forgotten what all this was like. I've been getting stagnant, sticking to a handful of friends-with-benefits types with whom the banter has somewhat stopped, as has the flirting.

"I've never been too much for hotel rooms, though," Finn says, tilting his head from side to side.

"No?"

"They're a little impersonal. My place is homey. There's a fireplace, a spa..."

I shift a little, coming closer. "Mm, but like you said, my hotel is closer..."

"I drive."

I didn't expect *where to go* to be the issue I'd have the most trouble with. I pull back a little, saying, "I don't know... we just met," hoping to make him think I'll back all the way out.

Finn's hand slides back from my thigh, almost off me, to the tip of my knee. "It's up to you."

Either have him at his place or not at all. *Dammit.*

Well, one way is a definite failure. And the other is just a little risky. I lean towards him again. "Did you say spa?"

Chapter Three

I scrunch up the earpiece in my napkin while he pays, then toss both in the bin on the way back to the entrance.

Once we're out under the marble pavilion, the valet goes to get his car. I hug my arms around myself as Finn turns to face me. "No jacket?"

No. They thought my pointy nipples might move things along a bit faster. "Left it in the office."

Reaching out, Finn pulls me to him. I let him, my heart picking up a little as I come up against a warm, hard torso, and I have to look up at his face, even in my heels. No sooner have our bodies connected than he leans down, not fast, just slow enough that if I want to back out I can, and since I don't, he kisses me.

There's a faint woody taste on his tongue from the scotch. His mouth is hot, slow and soft. I inhale and arch against him, opening my mouth, sliding my tongue against his.

By the time he pulls back, I feel as though I could float all the way to his bed. "Warmer?" he asks.

I lean into him. "Mm, still a little chilly."

But he doesn't have time to kiss me again because the valet has brought his car.

Before I ripped out the earbud, I could hear Theo scrambling with Melvin to organise and follow us. As Finn holds the door open for me now, I glance towards the wide avenue passing in front of the lounge, but I see nothing. Which is a good thing, I reason with myself, because if I see something, Finn might too.

The drive is less than ten minutes. The inside of his car is warm, almost lulling, and the music slow and sensual. I try not to glance at the rear-view mirror, though I sometimes get the impression of headlights behind us.

They could pull us over now. Part of me wishes they would. Now that I'm here and alone with Finn, I'm torn between actual attraction and a big helping of fear ingrained by all the warnings Theo gave me. Plus the fact they basically had to blackmail someone—me—into being the bait on this particular mission. I'm sure at least part of the reason is that I'm more disposable to them than one of their own.

But I know they won't make their move now. Theo seems like the kind of guy who likes to stick to the plan, even if I'm making that difficult.

No, they're going to wait until we're in his room, some of our clothes on the floor, his hands on me... I shift and straighten in my seat. I'm getting carried away, and we're only just pulling into his underground parking.

After the car pulls to a stop, Finn tilts his head to look at me. I give him my most alluring smile.

"Ready?" he asks.

"Of course."

Once out of the car, Finn takes my hand, leading me towards the elevator. This time of night, we're the only people about, so it arrives quickly, and when he pulls me inside, he presses the button in the same motion as pulling me between his body and the mirrored wall.

My breath catches as Finn presses against me. My hands slide up his shoulders, underneath his soft lambskin jacket. Hands gripping my waist as the elevator starts to ascend, he leans down faster this time, grazing his lips over mine and sending electricity across my skin before kissing me again. I arch up against his hard, warm body, and in turn, he presses me back.

I hardly notice when the elevator pings and the doors slide open into a wide corridor with a royal blue runner.

"Mm." Finn pulls back just a little, his eyes dark on my lips. I try not to gulp. My heart feels like it's speeding up too much. It's so easy to forget this is not a normal date.

Once inside his apartment, I expect Finn to turn the lights on, but instead, I find my lower back against the kitchen island as his short beard grazes my neck, a counter to his soft lips on the delicate skin of my throat. I make myself press back on his shoulders.

We're just a handful of blocks from the hotel I was supposed to take him to. Theo has surely worked out how to raid this apartment instead. "Bedroom?" I murmur, knowing there will be a window there.

Tugging my blouse out of where it's tucked into my skirt, Finn at first seems not to hear me, and I almost forget I said anything as he slides his hand over the bare skin of my ribs. My head tips back. This time, his teeth graze under my ear, too. His touch is luxurious. His fingers graze the bottom of my bra.

I force myself back to the land of reason, squeezing his arm. "I want you," I breathe, and it's not entirely untrue, but it is a better way to get him to the bedroom, where I can hopefully send the signal from.

It works. I step out of my heels as Finn pulls me towards the far end of the apartment. The bedroom is somewhat better lit. Partly, I see with relief, because of the large window. The blinds are open, looking straight out over the city and other dark skyscrapers.

One of which I'm willing to bet Agents Theo and Melvin are either watching from right now or on their way to. Can they get here instead of the hotel room? How long would it take?

I'm having trouble caring as Finn pushes me back onto the wide bed, falling on top of me. My skirt rides up around my hips as Finn slides between my legs, pressing me down and my legs apart. Hand sliding up my outer thigh, his fingers hook in the side of my G-string and tug it down my legs. I moan softly as he pulls it all the way off, tossing it off the bed. When he leans back, I half-sit to pull his shirt off, which he kneels to accommodate. The brief glimpse I get of his bare torso looks as good as it feels. Shirt off, Finn fits himself neatly flush over me again. I link my ankles behind his back, lifting against him to press against his telling bulge.

I run my hands and my nails suggestively up his back as his hot breath hits my ear, my throat. His lips trail down to my collarbone as he tugs my blouse open. "Mm, you're so sexy," he murmurs against me.

I close my eyes. How easy it would be to let this go, to just enjoy… but no, I know Theo, or whoever, is probably watching this whole thing. I need to do as they say. *For the money*, I remind myself. I can find sexy, seductive and alluringly dangerous men anywhere, right?

I press back on his bare shoulders. "You should get the curtains," I say, making sure to put extra husk into my voice.

This time there's no delay in his reaction. He straightens his arms to frame me, looking down at me. In the dark, it's hard to read his expression. "That's a shame."

"What?" I frown. That seems like an odd thing to say. But he has already slid off me.

I prop up to watch him walk to the window and let down the blinds.

And that's it. That's the signal. They'll be on their way now. My scalp prickles. I ignore it. Finn is lingering by the window. A laugh in my voice, I ask, "Well, are you coming back?"

Without a word, Finn walks back over, leaning over to flick a dim lamp on. Then he wastes no time in getting back on top of me.

There's something odd, though. Something changed, but I can't put my finger on it. He nestles between my legs, weighing me down, his forearms on either side of my head. I wait for him to kiss me.

He doesn't.

Instead, Finn ducks down, breath against my ear. "Are they watching from anywhere else?"

My eyes pop open. I try to wriggle, to see his face. But he has the advantage there. "What?" I ask, again, with an impression of a laugh, though it's more strained this time. I have a sinking feeling.

"Do they still have eyes in the room?" Finn lifts his head now, looking down at my face. His tone is so casual, it's disarming.

I can see he's deadly serious. And that he knows.

Tilting his head briefly, Finn goes on in a matter-of-fact way, "I just want to know if I still need to go through with fucking you. Obviously, I'm more than happy to. But I don't want to feel guilty afterwards if just some making out would have done, you know?" he adds, smirking a little.

"I don't know what you're talking about," I say. But even to me, my tone isn't right. I try to edge backwards.

Raising an eyebrow, Finn lets a little more of his weight onto me, keeping me trapped underneath him, my legs open around him in a way that lets my sex brush the front of his pants. "Come on, a woman in a bar, approaching a random guy? A man came up with that play, right?"

My eyes narrow at him. He's mocking me. He knew the whole time. Or at least suspected. "We like to imagine that kind of thing, but it never actually happens." Finn adds, "And if it did... would you really care about open curtains by then?"

I keep my lips closed against calling him a few choice words. He knows. It's over. Now just for how I get myself out of this because he's surely got a plan for my would-be saviors as well. Else he wouldn't be acting so damned confident. Amused, even.

Then his eyes dip to my chest, or, more accurately, my buttons. He takes a little of his weight off me, which blessedly stops the slight rubbing against my labia since my body is slower to get the message that it's not happening. So is his, by the feel.

"What have they got on you?" Eyes back to my face, Finn asks, "They threatened your family?"

I break eye contact. Tilting his head, Finn only looks closer at me, his mouth curving into a smile. "No, nothing so noble, is it?" he muses. "Money...." Grinning around the word, adding, "You were going to fuck a criminal for money?"

Finally, I can't help myself but to bite back. The silent route isn't working out so well for me. "None of your business."

Another soft laugh. "There may be hope for us yet. Now, tell me where their hidden camera is."

"Or what?"

"Or I'll have to strip you. And I don't think you want to be dragged out of here naked."

I grit my teeth. "Third button."

There's a short jerk. The button is off. He lays it on the bed, the tiny camera inside facing down. If they missed it, they'll just think I'm still pressed against him, and he none the wiser.

"Now get off me."

To my surprise, he does lift off me, taking his heat and weight and torturous pressure with him. But he stays hovering over me, one leg between mine, his hands weighing mine down into the bed.

Meeting his eye, I half-shrug. "Well then, what are you going to do with me?"

"That depends."

"On what?"

"On how much more you lie to me."

I think of making a break for it. His hands are soft now, but I'm sure they won't stay that way the moment I make any attempt at escape. "Try me," I say.

"Why are you doing this for them?"

"Like you said. Money."

He leans forward a little, hands squeezing my wrists. The sudden pressure between my legs makes me gasp. "I know they're on their way. It's in your interest to make this quick."

My jaw tightens, my pulse quickening. "They threatened to empty my offshore account."

He eases up. "And in what trade did you fill that account?"

I can tell what he's alluding to, what most people might assume a girl like me made her income doing. And that would probably be a better answer in my current situation, but something tells me he'll smell the lie.

Really, did he have to take my underwear off? I tell the truth. "Private investigator."

"I see." I don't like that tone. "And what do you know about me?"

"You give fake IDs to bad people."

"And?"

"Finn is your real name. You've been in the business a long time, evolving from fraudulent stolen IDs to making them yourself."

Finn's smile then is not reassuring. "That's enough."

"Enough for what?"

But he's off me, pulling me to my feet beside the bed. I glance around for my underwear, but by the time I spot it, Finn has grabbed his shirt and is pulling me towards the door. "Hey!"

"You don't need them."

"That's a matter of opinion. And don't need them *for what?*" My eyes narrow, though he's not looking at me. Rather, he has a firm hold on my wrist and has led me back into the dark kitchen. Grabbing my shoes, handbag, and his jacket from the counter, Finn wastes no time in then shoving me back in the other direction down the short corridor.

At the end, the narrow metal door of a service elevator awaits us. I'm willing to bet that's not in the official plans. Meaning Theo will miss it. And, more importantly, meaning that Finn is planning to take me somewhere. Which is not good.

"I'm not going with you!" I tug backwards.

"You are."

"What? Why?"

Finn takes the time to face me in the narrow hallway. "Let's call you collateral for now, Elsie."

"What's that supposed to mean?" I feel cold.

"You're a private investigator, aren't you? What could you tell them about me from our brief but pleasant time together?" Finn points out. "More than the average person. I can't let you back into their hands." The elevator slides open silently at the press of the button, revealing a small interior barely big enough for three people. He goes on, "Also, I need a safety net they're afraid to shoot through." I want to disagree with him there. I don't think they'd care when it came to him, or me. "Consider this the latest of your fresh employment opportunities," Finn comments with no small degree of sarcasm.

I stumble into the elevator as he pushes me. Turning to face him, I sneer, "If I know too much, it's only because you talk too much. And I can't tell them anything..."

A click. I look down. My hands are in cuffs. Where was he hiding those? His jacket, I suppose. It's folded over his arm. When I look up, he's smirking. I'm really starting not to like this guy. He doesn't even seem very rattled. "Are you serious?" I ask, lifting my cuffed hands.

"Afraid so."

"I think I'm the one who should be concerned here." The elevator is rattling softly on its descent.

"I'm taking you somewhere safe."

"Safe for me? Or for you?"

His smile turns a little meaner.

The single door rolls open as we come to a jerky stop.

We're looking out into a car park. But not the one he parked in earlier. A different car park, further down, lit with flickering bulbs. There are two duffel bags waiting beside the elevator.

"Do you just... leave these here?" I ask as he grabs them with one hand and the chain between my wrists with the other as he steps out and makes for a low, black car.

"What can I say? You learn a thing or two in this business." Tossing the duffel bags into the back seat, Finn walks around to the boot. I think he's going to pull something out of it, at best some kind of burner phone, at worst some guns. But it's empty

"I'd like to say I'm sorry about this..."

"About what?" The last word is muffled as he presses duct tape across my mouth. Before I can rip it off, there's also a bag over my head. Finn manhandles me, although somewhat gently, into the boot before slamming it closed.

As the engine starts up, I close my eyes, not that it makes much of a difference in the absolute darkness, and appreciate how thoroughly fucked I am. This did not go as planned. On the plus side, I haven't gotten murder vibes from Finn. I've been in situations like this—although less dire—with people who were more worrying.

I roll a little as the car pulls up an incline to exit the car park. And here I thought the van would be the worst ride in the back of a vehicle for my night.

***

What feels like an hour later, the boot comes open.

"Fucking asshole!" I curse as Finn grabs my arm and hauls me out of the trunk. "What the hell? Do you just have a kidnapping kit at the ready?"

"I see you managed to get the duct tape off," he muses, pulling the bag off my head. I blink in the light.

The interior we're in is huge, some kind of disused hangar, the ceiling a handful of stories high, light filtering down from hanging metal fixtures and tall fogged-glass windows. At the far end, which is really quite far considering we're technically indoors, past some vague re-purposed machines, are stacked containers with frames built around them to turn them into living spaces.

"Where the hell..."

Another man appears from behind a rusty iron device that looks like it used to have a part in making cars. "Zahir!" Finn calls to him, smiling. Zahir is slight for a man, with glossy black hair and thick eyelashes, his skin a deep, smooth bronze. He's wearing stained coveralls, his expression disarmingly sweet as he clasps Finn's hand. "Finn. New friend?"

I sneer at him. He can obviously see that I'm cuffed and just came out of the boot of a car. He smiles widely back, with straight white teeth.

"Something like that. The feds sent her after me."

"Oh?" He raises an eyebrow. But not too much, not enough to suggest this is unheard of. I guess he must be part of Finn's fake ID business, a co-worker or the like. "They're getting serious." Then he turns his big brown eyes on me. "What are you going to do with her?"

"For now, she's insurance."

Zahir tilts his head. "Smart. The collateral would look bad for them if..."

"Can you not talk about me like I'm not here?" I inquire.

"Good point. Zahir, get Bridget to do a search on Elsie here for me. She's a private investigator, that's all I know so far. And her name, obviously."

Nodding, Zahir says with a level of confidence that worries me, "That's all Bridget needs."

I resist groaning. Finn having more information about me is really all I need.

"In the meantime, I guess you're needing the lot?"

"Yeah. Where's safe?"

Zahir considers. He has a dirty cloth in his hands, which he idly wipes his palms with. I guess he works on machinery when he's not engaging in criminal activities. "The Peninsula safe house, maybe. But not tonight. Stay here for now. The Turkish couple are still in the apartment for now, but the Pad is free."

"That's fine. I want to keep her close."

I'll bet he does. Finn ducks down, and suddenly, I'm over his shoulder. "Thanks, Zahir!" he calls back as he carries me toward the container homes.

I thump at his back. "Hey, dickhead! I can walk!"

"But were you going to?"

Probably not, no.

***

For the inside of a container, the space is actually pretty homey, cute even. The bedroom is dominated by a double bed, with a closed-off area for an ensuite, and another container connects perpendicularly to add on a lounge and kitchen. The windows are cut out to line up with the windows of the hangar itself, and though they're fogged—preventing me from getting any idea of where we are—they do let light in from outside.

All this also means there's only one bed.

Not a girl to waste an opportunity, I linger in the bedroom. If I can get him dumb... I'm sure the window is breakable with the right amount of enthusiasm. I'll deal with the handcuffs and the lack of underwear later. If I can give Theo the location of this place, surely that will be enough for them to let me off. Then I can strut off into the sunset with my money safe and sound.

"I'll take the couch. If you try anything..."

"I don't have pajamas," I point out, turning to face him.

Finn raises an eyebrow, like he doubts that I even wear pajamas. I don't, but that's hardly the point. "Then sleep in that."

I blink, slowly. "Could I borrow your shirt?"

Finn's eyes narrow on me. After a moment of consideration, he sighs and pulls a small key out of his pocket. Before he unlocks the cuffs, he grips my wrist. "Don't try anything. Get the shirt on. These are going back on afterwards."

I nod innocently, the cuffs clicking to release. Shoving them with the key into his pocket, Finn pulls his shirt off, tossing it to me. I glance discreetly at his torso. He might be a criminal, but I can still appreciate a good physique, can't I?

I take his shirt, still warm, and lay it on the bed. He has to watch me, I know that, in case I try to stab him or something while his back is turned. I don't turn fully away as I unbutton my blouse, then unclip my bra, making sure my small sigh of relief has an audible quality. When I toss it on the bed, I know he can see the silhouette of my breasts. Then I fumble with his shirt, bending down to pick it up.

"I know what you're doing."

Turning to fully face him, I'm gratified to see his eyes draw down to my breasts. "What am I doing?"

Gaze dragging back upwards, Finn glares at me. "Just put the damn shirt on."

Instead, I step towards him. He straightens but doesn't back away. "If we're going to be stuck together anyway..." I begin suggestively.

"I'm warning you..."

Up on my toes, I brush my lips over his. I feel his mouth relax against mine, sliding my hands up to his shoulders. After a moment, I feel his hands weigh on my hips, pulling me just a bit closer, his head leaning down just a bit further. I arch against him. Catching my wrists, Finn pulls my hands behind my back, pulling me flush against him. It's working! Now I just need to...

A click. Cold metal on my wrists. My gratification comes to a sharp end. I'm cuffed.

Our lips break apart as I realise what he's done. I blink. "Bastard!"

Finn steps back, grabs his shirt off the bed, and pulls it over my head and arms. "I warned you not to try anything."

A few choice words from me follow him out of the room.

And now I need to sleep with my hands cuffed behind my back.

***

By the time I get to sleep, awkwardly twisted and with aching shoulders, it's not long before dawn is lighting up the windows and Finn comes in to inform me that it's time to go.

This time, when he takes off the cuffs, I don't try anything. I'm too tired, anyway. Which may have been his thinking. Finn stands outside the bathroom door while I make what attempt I can at refreshing myself and putting on yesterday's clothes.

Shortly, we're back at the car, though this time there's suitcases in the back, and I'm guessing we've been refueled enough to go long distance. I wonder where Theo and Melvin are looking. If they're even looking. How much they're cursing my impulsive choice to go to Finn's place. Surely not as much as *I'm* cursing my impetuousness.

As Finn re-cuffs my hands, I glare at him and say the first thing I've said all morning. "You could have at least gotten me fresh clothes."

"Why?" he asks. "No one can smell you in the trunk."

Chapter Four

With my hands cuffed in front of me this time, and a pillow added to the boot, I actually doze off in the back. Which, consequently, gives me enough anger to fume for the rest of the trip.

By the time Finn pulls me out of the boot, having not bothered to gag me this time, I wrench away from him, stumble with a little dizziness, and curse at him. "Was that really necessary? You've got tinted fucking windows!"

Then I realise where we are.

"The *woods*?" I take a cautious step backwards. I could have been wrong about the murderous tendencies, after all.

Finn sighs. "Don't get the wrong idea. There's a perfectly ordinary house down that path. It's just... out of service range."

I give him a look. "You've brought me, in the trunk of a car, hand-cuffed, to the middle of the woods and then you tell me we're off the grid, and *now* you think I'm getting the wrong idea?"

Finn seems to realise that's a tall order. He holds his hands up. "Let's just remind ourselves that you got yourself into this mess."

"Actually, I think that was you, too."

Finn's eyes narrow. "You were trying to trick me into having sex with you so that your buddies could arrest me and let you keep your barely legally gotten gains. Or am I missing something?"

"The part where you're a criminal. And my 'gains' are perfectly legitimately gotten!"

Shaking his head, Finn shrugs. "You can argue until the cows come home." I glance around. Are there cows here? I don't have a wealth of experience with livestock. "But in the end, I have the keys, and you're wearing the cuffs, and we're going down that path to a house where I will *not* murder you." He turns away to yank open the back door and starts hauling out suitcases.

I want to kick him. Instead, I patiently ask, "Is this really your plan? To drag me everywhere with you in the hopes that they like me well enough not to bomb you or something else equally bizarre?"

Finn glances back at me out of the open door. "As bizarre as sending you?"

"I'm a reasonable choice," I sneer. "Now answer the question."

Shrugging, Finn reaches further into the back seat, gathering loose items of clothing into the suitcase he has open. "Every plan is good until it stops working. Then, I'll consider a new tactic."

"And what tactic is that?"

"Something more... shall we say, aggressive."

That doesn't sound beneficial to me. I narrow my eyes at him. "Have they tried this before?"

"With a woman as bait? No. This is a new low."

"You're one to talk. They wouldn't go to the trouble if you weren't giving fake IDs to drug lords."

With two suitcases outside the car now, he closes the car door, locking it manually. I guess it's an older model of car, something without so many electronic and trackable bits. "That's what they told you, huh?" Finn asks, meeting my eye.

"I saw you myself! In the lounge, with that creeper."

One suitcase under his arm, the other in the same hand, Finn pulls me none too gently by the arm. "Have it your way. Come on, it's getting late."

I shut my mouth and let myself be led.

***

The house is more of a cottage, sitting on the edge of a wide valley which, while bare, is at least a less worrying backdrop than the woods. Inside, the fixtures look to be about two decades old, but they work, and the place is decorated in a taste that reminds me of my grandmother, which, all things considered, is a comforting aspect.

Then Finn shows me to my room.

"You're putting me in *here*? It's a broom closet!"

"There's a chicken coop out the back if you'd prefer."

"I suppose you're also planning to starve me like an orphan you keep under the stairs."

Watching Finn's face, I can tell it's just occurring to him that neither of us has eaten since a dry muesli bar at breakfast, wolfed down on the way out of the hideout. "Shit."

***

These criminal types are surprisingly considerate. A fully stocked kitchen awaits us at the back of the house, overlooking a long green yard tinted in orange with the setting sun. Or rather, it awaits Finn, seeing as, in light of all the knives and other sharp implements I could grasp while his back is turned, he cuffs my hands to the heavy dining chair I'm sitting on.

I can't remember the last time I had a man cook for me. This was certainly not how I imagined it happening again. At least it smells good.

"Can I have a book or something?"

Finn doesn't turn around from where he's slicing onions. "Sure."

I stare at his back and jiggle the chain between my cuffs. "Can you *get* me one?"

Glancing over his shoulder, he gives me that progressively more and more irritating grin. "Oh, do you not have one?"

I sneer. "Must have forgotten to slip one into my skirt. Speaking of which, do I get fresh clothes, ever? And underwear."

"We'll see."

I roll my eyes and stare out the window instead. A hare nibbles at the grass by the tree line. "How long are we going to stay here?"

"A couple days, until somewhere else comes up. Or until your buddies manage to trace us."

"They're not my buddies."

"Your employers."

"Also wrong."

Our bickering is brought to an end by Finn putting a bowl of steaming food in front of me. It smells delicious. Taking his own seat, Finn puts a fork—just a fork, no knife—within my reach. Leaning over, he unlocks my hands from around the chair but then re-cuffs them.

Awkwardly, with my hands chained together, I eat a few hot mouthfuls, enough that my stomach no longer feels like a hollow cave, and then the cuffs return to being my major irritation.

Looking up at Finn, who is quietly enjoying his own meal, I ask, "Are these really necessary?" Holding my hands up. "I don't have some secret woodswoman skills. Where the hell am I going to go?"

Finn tilts his head. "You strike me as the resourceful type."

I sigh, glancing out the window again. It's fully dark now. "I'd like to have a shower."

"I'll bet."

I cross my arms on the table, as best I can, and lean towards him a little, my missing button revealing my bra, which has got to be worth something, even if I do smell. "You can watch if it makes you feel better."

Finn sits back. "Trying that again, huh?"

"Well, what else are we supposed to do here?" I straighten. "I'm guessing we're not gonna be hiking buddies." I smile. "We may as well pass the time in some *other* kind of entertaining way."

Chuckling, Finn raises an eyebrow. "You're definitely not one of those only-have-sex-for-love types, huh?"

Shrugging, I say, "If it feels good, what's the harm?"

Eyes narrowing, he asks, "Weren't you a PI for suspicious spouses? Seems like it can do harm, then, doesn't it?"

Great, I guess he did manage to find more information on me, or his friends did, anyway. I'm not a fan of the use of past tense in his words. "I still am a PI. And that's different. Are *you* married?"

Finn snorts. "No."

"How shocking."

Finn stands, taking our empty bowls to the sink. I glance over my shoulder as he opens a high cupboard and finds a dusty bottle of wine. "Well, we could drink instead," he muses.

"That'll do."

***

I take the first sip, pause, then swallow. "Well, it's not the best thing I've ever tasted."

Finn seems to agree. "Beggars can't be choosers, I guess."

I sit back, hitching my elbow over the corner of my chair. I know it reveals my bra, and the way I bring one leg up shows a lot of my bare thigh, but I'm not in a mood to care. "So, why do your buddies own a place like this? It doesn't strike me as an abode for drug dealers or whatnot."

Finn takes his time having another sip and manages not to pull too much of a face as he stares into the crystal wineglass. "It is what it looks like. A family home."

"So, it's less obvious?" I ask. "Or... I guess traffickers and the like have families too sometimes."

Finn stares at me. "You don't get it."

"Then explain it to me."

"Why?"

I shrug. "Why not? We're both stuck here."

Finn snorts. "You had a very similar justification for having sex earlier."

"Hey, that still stands, too." The wine is dulling my irritation. And doing the other thing which wine does to me, which is that it makes me a little... sensual.

Finn rolls his eyes. "Families do stay here sometimes. Just not the type you're imagining."

"I get it," I say, shrugging. "You want to make yourself feel better about your 'job'. Really, that's fine..."

Finn's tone tells me I've struck a nerve or otherwise irritated him more than usual. "And what about your job? You enjoy being the bearer of bad news?"

I stiffen. "I'm helping people discover the truth."

"You're benefitting from their misfortune."

I glare at him across the table. "I'm saving them time. It always comes out sooner or later."

"Wow."

"Wow, what?" I ask, too quickly.

"Nothing," Finn says, shaking his head, "Just that you must have had some real shit boyfriends." Then he tilts his head in that overly observant, bordering on empathetic way, the same look he gave me before he guessed that I was in this for money. "Or shitty parents."

I shift. "Shut up. This isn't a counselling session."

"Hey, whole world's got daddy issues."

"Oh yeah? What was yours? Car thief? Money launderer?"

"Actually, he worked in a factory until he died," he tells me, followed by a dry, humorless chuckle.

I sigh. This conversation has not gone the way I was planning. "I should go to bed."

"That's probably a good idea."

I stand too fast. The wine hits me harder than I expected. I'm holding the wineglass, and it sloshes a little as I struggle to catch myself with my hands cuffed. Finn is there, his hands on my arms, righting me. Then he grins down at me. "Lightweight?"

He's standing close, his hands still brushing my arms. I bite my lip and smile. "Not usually."

Taking the wineglass out of my hands, he reaches past me to put it on the table. As he's drawing back, I turn my head to catch his lips with mine. I feel his intake of breath, but he doesn't pull away. He tastes sweeter than the wine on his lips. Hands gripping my arms, he dips lower, tasting me back.

I sway backwards, urging him to press against me, so I can feel his body through our clothes. I pull back long enough to loop my arms over his shoulders, his hands coming to my waist. The table presses against my butt, and as Finn's mouth traces my chin, I edge up onto it, opening my legs around his hips so he fits neatly against me.

Finn plants his hands on either side of my hips, chest leaning into mine, pushing me backwards enough that I need to hitch my knee over his hip to help myself stay upright. Staying close, he looks into my eyes. "You really want this?"

In answer, I take his hand and guide it up my thigh until his fingers brush my labia, my wetness. A low sound comes from the back of his throat, and he claims my mouth again, his hand gripping high on my thigh. Pushing me down to my back, he leans over me, weighing on me.

"I'm not uncuffing you," he murmurs around my mouth.

"Kinky," I breathe. Because at the moment, I don't care. I probably will later, but that's later.

I grip his shirt until my hands are fists, arching my back to press up against him. His weight feels divine, the hard table under my back leaving no recourse from it. I feel light from the wine and heavy with need at once.

"Is this a bad time to mention that I don't have condoms?"

Managing to think of something other than the heat between my legs for a second, I eye him. "Talk about unprepared."

"I wasn't exactly preparing for *this*. That would be creepy."

I guess he's right there. What would I have thought if he actually had them? "Whatever, I have an IUD," I say, wriggling against him.

His hands are pushing my skirt higher until it's almost just a band around my hips. I push his jeans down with my feet, seeing as my hands are trapped, looped over his shoulders, until he helps and frees himself.

Voice a husky whisper, Finn tells me, "Last chance to change your mind."

"Shut up and fuck me," I tell him back.

He half-groans, half-laughs, burying his face in the side of my neck, his teeth nipping as he directs himself, the head of his cock pressing me open. I bite my lip, arching to pull him deeper, and he obliges, pressing against me, sliding slowly deeper and deeper until I'm gasping, gripping him through his shirt. Finn's breath is hot against my ear, his groan mingling with my own long, audible sigh of pleasure.

I hitch my leg over his hip, and he presses down on my other side with his hand as he thrusts, filling me completely. Mouth open, I gasp around the sensation, the deep pleasure taking the control out of my limbs and my voice. He hasn't even started moving yet, and I'm already high.

Finn rolls his hips against mine. I cry out and roll with him, meeting his thrusts when he speeds up. Grunting, he presses one of my wrists to the table above my head, and seeing as my hands are still cuffed, both of my arms end up pinned. I bite my lip, reveling in the sensation of restraint, letting it take me to the edge.

I tighten and clamp around him, and Finn curses softly, "Fuck."

"Don't stop," I gasp, eliciting him to curse again, but he keeps going, keeps his pace, and soon I'm there, panting until I moan, crying out as the climax takes hold of me.

Face buried against my neck, Finn rides it out as I clench and clamp around him, helplessly vulnerable to the pleasure which makes me cry out as though in pain. As it subsides, he grunts, thrusting longer and harder, his hand on my wrist gripping hard enough to bruise.

Finn's orgasm crashes over the aftershocks of mine. I feel it fill me, as though it is me climaxing again. I grip him, rolling up against him even when his own movement loses its rhythm, and he falls, empty and complete, over me.

Chapter Five

I wake up in an unfamiliar room. The quilt is pale pink with white flowers that have bright orange centers, tiny bees filling in the spaces between. A rooster crows somewhere, bright dawn light coming through the dainty floral curtains.

My head hurts. I roll.

I'm naked. And so is Finn.

At the sight of his sleeping face, I roll heavily back to where I was, staring at the ceiling. "Well, that was a bad idea," I mutter to myself. But then, remembering the sex, I have to appreciate that it wasn't a *totally* bad idea.

I wait for a beat. How are my hands *still* cuffed? I glance across him, at the bedside table. Cuff keys would be good. Car keys would be great. Unfortunately, neither is in plain view so far. There is a drawer, however. Up on my elbow, I watch his sleeping face. He could be faking sleep. But to what end?

I could get out of bed, walk around. But in a house this old, I just know the floorboards creak. I sit up a little more. If I can avoid touching him... a difficult feat with one's hands tied, but I manage to lean over him, propping my hands on the far edge of the bed, beside him. Now just a bit of core work and I can reach the bedside table and...

"Do I need to ask what you're looking for?"

I gasp, losing my delicate balance, my hands coming heavily back to the bed. I look down at Finn's face, his grey eyes watching me from below. He's quite nice from this angle, too. I can only imagine the view he's getting, with my breasts over his head.

I pull back, kneeling now. "Just checking for soap."

"Uh-huh." Finn props up. Glancing around the room, last night seems to come back to him too. "Well, this just got messier."

***

We're back at the dining table for a breakfast of cereal, and from the quiet, thoughtful way that Finn eats his muesli, I think it's a pretty good guess that he's thinking about what we did on this table last night.

It probably doesn't help that I'm still wearing the same handcuffs and also his shirt.

"So, what's the plan today?" I ask Finn, drawing him out of his reverie. When he looks at me, I let my lips curve in a smirk.

"There is no plan. This is what hiding out looks like. Being bored."

"Hm." I raise an eyebrow at him. "Something wrong...?"

Finn holds my eye a beat. "We shouldn't have done that... I shouldn't have done that last night."

It takes me a moment to realise what he's getting at. He fills in the blanks, anyway. "You're in a vulnerable position. I'm in the position of power."

I resist telling him I was exactly in the position I wanted to be in, saying instead, "We're both adults. I made it pretty clear what I wanted."

"And why did you want it?"

I laugh. "You know, I don't usually have to tell men they're pretty the morning after—"

"I don't like being slept with for ulterior motives," Finn says simply, cutting me off.

"And I don't like *sleeping with people for ulterior motives*," I state back. "And I didn't." When he only looks at me, I point out, "You've got some trust issues, you know?"

That finally breaks the serious expression he's been holding all morning. Sighing, he sits back. "Alright, fine. You were horny. That's it. We're not doing it again."

"Whatever you say."

"Elsie..." his voice warns. Apparently, I wasn't convincing enough.

Raising my hands as though in surrender, I promise, "I solemnly swear not to drink more wine."

*****

The truce lasts until about lunchtime.

"Look, whether or not anyone is going to be near enough to smell me, I need to shower," I tell Finn.

I'm more gratified than I should be as Finn leans against the bathroom sink and watches me undress. I can feel him trying not to watch. Which makes encouraging him to watch even more satisfying. The loose pants he's thrown on don't go a long way to hiding anything. He's holding my cuffs and the key to them.

Once I've gone through the extended process of getting all my clothes off, I take my time in the shower. I leave the door open so that he knows I'm not 'up to no good,' as I soap myself. Part of the joy is actually relishing the feel of the hot water after a handful of days without a shower, and the other part is torturing Finn, given that he's decided we're only having sex the one time. I can't resist a challenge.

"You already soaped that part."

I open my eyes as his voice reaches me through the falling water. I look back over my shoulder. "How do you know?" I look straight at his erection, which is making itself known through his track pants.

"Are you almost done?"

"Why?" I ask, turning my face into the water, closing my eyes as it washes over me. "You bored? Got other places to be?"

He's quiet, and I think he's given up and gone back to silent sulking. But then I gasp, almost jump, as hands come to my hips, sliding over my wet skin. I go to turn, but Finn holds me where I am, his bare body coming up against the back of mine, the water running down both of us.

Head dipping down, he traces the top of my shoulder with his lips.

I already feel like melting. "You shouldn't tease," he murmurs.

"Mm," I sigh, pressing back, saying, "So sorry," in a way that leaves no doubt that I'm not.

Hand sliding up my back, Finn pushes me to bend forward. My hands come to the shower shelf, gripping as I arch and press towards him, inviting him.

Taking the invite, Finn bumps my feet apart with his, and as my legs come wider, I feel deliciously vulnerable. His hand slides back down and over my butt, then keeps going.

Sliding his hand between my thighs, he cups me from behind. I wriggle, breath already heavy as his fingers part me, then push inside me. My hair hangs down like wet rope, his hand moves smoothly, small movements that nonetheless make me gasp and want to bounce back on them.

When he takes his hand away, I'm disappointed, but not for long, as soon something else is taking its place. Entering me slowly from behind, Finn grips my hip with one hand, his other on the back of my neck.

The new angle makes me cry out immediately, shifting back and higher as he pushes deep in small thrusts. I can feel my heart skipping, the pleasure spreading out through my belly and all the way to my toes. I forget about the water, about my mission, even about what he is to me, and just move with him, bouncing back as we find a rhythm, my knees weak with the building need of it.

To my own surprise as well, I think, as his, something about the angle is stroking just the right way, and I orgasm suddenly, against my own control. I need to grip the shelf as it powers through my limbs, making me weak and tense at once, my cries muffled by the shower.

I still moan and gasp even as it recedes, and Finn lets himself go, thrusting deeper than ever, his hand now gripping the shelf beside mine. I can see his knuckles, see the tension, then watch as it leaves him with release.

***

The dress is long and flowy, cinched around my waist with a tie. It's not quite my style, on the conservative end and leaning towards county-fair wife, but given how comfortable it turns out to be, I'm thinking it could *become* my style.

Once it's on, I look up at Finn, his hair still damp as he pulls on faded jeans. "Underwear?" I inquire.

Looking skyward, he pretends to think as he does up his buttons. "Hm, must have slipped my mind."

Prick.

The cuffs don't go back on, for now. Finn also doesn't provide me with shoes, so I guess he's reasoned that I can't go very far anyway, what without underwear or shoes and being in the middle of nowhere.

As for keys to the car, and my best means of escape, I expect they're locked away in a safe somewhere.

"Was this it?" I ask, pinching the skirts of my dress.

"No, Zahir packed you a few other things."

"I'll just take them, then," I say. I hardly need Finn to keep a hold of my wardrobe.

"Take them?"

"To my room. Remember? The broom closet."

"You're staying in here."

I laugh. "Listen, just because we had sex, there's no need to go all domestic…"

"I'd prefer you where I can keep an eye on you." Finn smiles. "So really, this works out well," he quips, walking past me on his way to the hall. "You did insist on having sex again."

I close my mouth. My intention had not been to make this easier *on him*. "I don't like to share beds."

Pausing outside the door, he glances back over his shoulder. "No? You like being handcuffed to them?"

Under certain circumstances… but I know that's really not what he's implying.

***

Really, I've got nothing against sharing a bed. But sharing one with Finn should be weird. Which it is, but only because he puts track pants on and throws an oversized shirt at me across the bed.

I eye the bundle in my hand. "It's a little late for discretion, don't you think?"

He gives me a look. "I don't want you to think this is for my benefit. Now put it on."

I sigh and pull the shirt over my naked torso. Whatever helps him sleep at night, I guess. I've already been watching him clear the room of anything sharp, using his body to block the safe under the bed as he locked everything away behind a passcode.

I sit heavily on the bed, glancing back at him. "I guess you're not a cuddler."

Rather than answering me, he says, "I need to shave. Get some sleep."

It's dark outside already, the kind of pitch darkness that only occurs far away from city lights. As the ensuite door closes, leaving just a ring of light around it, I groan and lie down on my side of the bed. I could read. He has found me a small pile of vaguely modern books, but in truth, I am actually tired, and the urge to just close my eyes and let the day slide away turns out to be too great.

***

In that zone halfway between asleep and awake, I stir, unsure how long it's been. The bed next to me is still empty, the ring still around the ensuite door. But it's the door to the hallway that has drawn me awake. It clicks, then creaks softly as it opens.

Frowning, I sit up. "Finn? What were you doing out there?"

The features of the figure are lost to the darkness beyond what little light spills from under the bathroom door. Something has the hair on the back of my head rising, alertness coming fast.

I know the figure in the doorway isn't Finn. And there's not many reasons to be sneaking around a house at night picking locks.

I roll sharply to my right, tumbling off the bed and hitting the floor hard. A heavy thunk hits the pillow where I was. I hear a tumble and a curse. They've tripped over the suitcase. I edge sideways under the bed before I scream.

I can see the bottom of the ensuite door bang open, then I watch two sets of feet, one bare, one in soft black boots, scuffle. It's brief, briefer than it is in the movies. Then the feet in black are running out of the room. Finn chases but briefly. I hear a silenced shot. Something smashes.

I creep out from under the bed and try the safe. If it's not Finn that comes back, something sharp would sure be handy. But no luck. A creak that feels like it's right beside my ear has my heart stopping.

I breathe a sigh of relief as it turns out only to be Finn in the doorway. His chest is rising and falling fast.

"Are you alright?" he asks.

"I'm fine. Who the hell was that?" I ask, standing.

Finn's eyes cut to my side of the bed. Mine follow. There's a short silver knife sticking out of my pillow. "Oh," I say, feeling a little dizzy.

Finn pulls me down to sit on his side of the bed. I stare at my knee, at an old scar, an effort to focus on something small and real. Finn has crouched in front of the safe. He's opening it, pulling out a gun. "They ran off, across the field, before I could catch them. We're not leaving this room again tonight. You understand? I'll call Zahir. We're out of here in the morning."

I'm having trouble following him. "Why me? Why did someone try...?"

"I don't know. But they've gone now. I doubt they'll try again tonight. I'll keep watch." He's dropping the blinds, dimming the lights. Then he drags the heavy dresser in front of the door.

I should help. But I can't. "Why does someone want me dead?"

Shaking his head, Finn meets my eye. "I don't know. But they're willing to pay to have it done. I don't think either of us are safe here anymore."

***

The next day, Zahir doesn't have much of a better idea than we do.

The night passed at a snail's pace, but it did pass. I felt safer with the rising sun, which is ridiculous because people are murdered in broad daylight all the time.

Zahir sits on the couch. He arrived a couple of hours after sunrise. And, worryingly for me, he also looks concerned.

"Who knew where she was?" Finn asks.

Zahir spreads his hands. "Not many people. You, me. Bridget?"

Finn shakes his head. "Bridget wouldn't betray us."

"She did the search on her..." But then Zahir shakes his head. "You're right. There are the others—the ones that set up the safe house. Is anyone tapping your phone?"

At this, Finn looks at me. "Your friends?"

I shake my head, staring vacantly at the corner of the coffee table. "I don't think they'd try to have me killed. Why would they? Melvin is too by-the-book. I guess Theo —"

"Theo?" Fin cuts me off, staring at me like I've grown a second head. "*Big* Theo?"

I frown. "You know a cop?"

He runs a hand over his forehead. "Not for a long time. We grew up together, kind of."

"Come again? You're brothers?" I ask, sounding as incredulous as I feel.

"My dad fostered him. He was in the system."

I can hardly believe what I'm hearing. "Well, what the hell happened? Is hunting you down his way of showing brotherly affection?"

He shrugs. "Knowing Theo, he probably thinks he's doing what's best for me. That it's better he has me in custody rather than someone who would actually hurt me." Finn gives me a pointed look. "You could say we went in different directions."

I snort. "Maybe not so different. If he's trying to have me killed to cover up his blunder."

Now he looks angry, and I realise what I've said. "You really think I'm like that..."

"All this aside..." Zahir interrupts before we can go any further.

He's right. This is not the time to let emotions run high. I spread my hands. "I don't have anything trackable on me, anyway. So I don't see how it could be him."

Zahir nods thoughtfully. "Whatever side of the law this is coming from, it's not safe here. You need something somewhere that having bodyguards doesn't raise suspicion. And somewhere very far away."

I look between the two of them. I get the feeling I'm not going to like this.

Chapter Six

"**D**ubai?" I ask. "Are you kidding me?" But I get the feeling they're not. Partly because I'm looking at the private plane. I can practically feel the air off of the engines as it powers up.

"Where did you have in mind?" Finn shouts to be heard, coming up next to me. He passes me something. I glance down and realise it's a passport. 'My passport,' but not really.

"Putting your skills to work?"

"Come on. It's time to board. Ever been on a private plane?" Finn asks, glancing back at me.

"No," I call after him, but he's out of earshot as I mutter, "And I didn't picture this being how it would happen."

***

Soon we're in the sky, with a twelve-hour-plus flight ahead of us. Of course, in this kind of comfort, I can hardly complain. At least there's probably no knife-wielding assassins up here. The champagne the silent hostess served as we boarded the flight was particularly soothing.

Finn is on his laptop, largely ignoring me. But I have to ask. "Why do you guys even own a private jet? Surely your clients can afford their own?"

He glances up at me. "It's a good way to get people out of places they don't want to be in."

"That they can't get out of themselves?" I ask.

I see the muscle in his jaw twitch. I can tell I annoy him every time the subject of what his work really is comes up. "Yes. *That they can't get out of themselves.*"

"I guess you add it to their bill."

The laptop closes with a definitive click. "Instead of trying to decipher the world of new identities, maybe your detective skills would be better put to use figuring out who wants you dead." Raising an eyebrow, he adds, "Or at least, who wants you dead *the most.*"

I pull a face at him. "How should I know? It's got to be one of your buddies who told them where to find me. Reason would suggest they're also the ones who hired our would-be assassin."

"I don't see it that way."

"You don't *see* it?" I ask, incredulous. "You work among criminals, and you don't see it?" I throw my hands up when he says nothing. "Maybe, just off the top of my head, someone offered them money!"

Finn's lips tighten, and he says nothing.

Turning on each other isn't helping. I top up two glasses of champagne and move over to the seat across from him, offering him one.

Taking it, Finn's expression softens a little. "You'll be safer in Dubai. We have contacts there. We can figure out what's going on."

I nod, taking another sip. But I'm not so convinced. It's a strange feeling, knowing someone out there is waiting to cross your name off a list.

"Give me your foot."

I blink. "Excuse me?"

"You look tense." Finn puts down his glass. "Give me your foot. I'll give you a massage." I raise an eyebrow, and he rolls his eyes. "Not like that."

I think of telling him no. But then, a foot massage doesn't sound half bad. I slip out of my sandal and delicately put my foot on his knee.

His hands are warm and sure. At first, it tickles, but his kneading is so firm I soon feel the stress relief he was talking about. I let out a long breath and sit back in my seat. "You're good at that."

"Hm."

Glancing out the window, I see the ocean passing by far, far below. As the tension seeps away, I feel the lack of sleep catching up with me. "How do you sleep on one of these things?"

"There's a bed back there." He nods toward the back of the plane, past some maroon curtains.

"Just the one?" I ask, as he indicates for my other foot. I oblige.

Finn smiles a little, pressing his thumb along the sole of my foot. "I can sleep out here if it makes you feel better."

"I wouldn't mind a massage in bed." Then I see his lips curve and realise what I said. "I didn't even mean that."

"I hear that's also good stress relief." He grins.

"Hm." I sip my champagne. "Tempting..."

***

I fall on top of him, straddling him on the bed.

But I don't stay there for long. Finn grabs me and rolls, putting me underneath him.

"You know we've never done it in a bed," I manage, in a spare moment that my mouth isn't somewhere on him.

Edging me higher up the bed, Finn tilts his head. "Maybe that's the secret. This could be terrible."

I snort. Unlikely.

Pushing my skirts higher up my hips, Finn settles over me. I wriggle my arms free of the sleeves, my hands coming back to his face as he kisses me again.

"Good thing you're not wearing underwear, huh?" Finn muses.

I roll my eyes, but it's hard to be angry at him when he's just taken his shirt off. And it is also nice to be thinking of something besides an assassin with, among other things, knives.

Finn's hands are planted on either side of my shoulders, and when I come free of the top half of my dress, he ducks down and catches my nipple with his teeth.

"Fuck," I gasp, hooking my knee over his hip so I can grind up on him, my hands making short work of opening his jeans and pushing them down along with his underwear.

Now that he's free, I run my fingers up his length. His tongue flicks, and I jolt and grip him, squeezing until I feel him moan against my breast. Weighing down on me, Finn's hand slides down to squeeze my butt, his body flush along the top of mine. Like that, he enters me.

Head tipping back, I forget about anyone else on the plane who could potentially be listening, letting myself go to the pleasure. I feel it reverberating through his body, his breath grunting into my hair as our hips roll together.

For a time, I can think of nothing else.

***

I'm in the wrong business.

Finn frowns at me, and I realise I said that out loud. We've just stepped out of the elevator. Into the penthouse. The two-story penthouse, with a central courtyard passing through both floors and open to the bright blue sky. The furniture is tasteful and oriental, the floor plan sprawling, open windows letting in a delicate breeze and a view over the city.

Finn puts down our measly two suitcases as I go to the balcony.

"We don't pay for this," he tells me.

I frown back at him. "Are we squatting?" I'm suddenly less comfortable. But no, we can't be—the security guards checked us downstairs.

"No, we just have friends here. In high places, you might say."

"How do you make a friend like that?" I ask, leaning on the railing to face him. "New IDs whenever he wants?"

"*She*, and not exactly. Seahorse did her and her family a favor some time ago."

I smile a little. "Why so cryptic?"

"Because you've already made your mind up about what we do."

"If I've been misled, explain it to me," I urge. There have been too many hints, too many annoyed looks whenever I mention his criminal activities.

Finn stares at me for a time, then sighs. "Tomorrow, we'll meet with Amina and see what she might know. But the day after that, I have somewhere I need to go. People I need to see. Come with me, and you'll get a better idea of what we do."

I frown. "What about my shadow?"

"We'll go in disguise. It won't take long. The only one who knows who we really are is Amina, the one who owns this place. And I'd trust her with my life."

I nod slowly. "You're not worried I'll run away?"

Finn smiles, tilts his head from side to side. "You could. But I think you know that right now you need me as much as I need you."

True enough. Somehow, we've become each other's safety net. My only hope of finding out who is trying to kill me is through Finn and Seahorse. And his best hope of Bici holding back on the firepower is if they're scared of making headlines by getting a woman they basically blackmailed killed.

I can't help but notice that in both situations, it's me with the potential for bodily harm.

But I agree anyway. "Okay. I'll go."

***

While nothing was explicitly said, and there's more than enough bedrooms in the penthouse, Finn and I sleep in the same room. Overlooking the pool and garden of the whole building, but high up enough to still be private, the room is huge, done in warm colours, a frame around the bed draped in flowy, pale-orange chiffons.

Given the circumstances, I shouldn't sleep well. But I do, partly because Finn is a cuddler. At least, once he falls asleep, he is. I resolve not to tell him of his nocturnal habit of chasing me across the bed until I'm firmly under his arm, the covers thrown back against the warm summer night air. It's cute, though I'm trying not to think of him as *cute*. Boyfriends are cute. Men you're effectively stuck with or you might die, and who happen to be good stress relief, are not.

This will be over as soon as it can be.

As the sun rises, I slide out of bed and into the ensuite overlooking our private courtyard. There's a silk robe, and I tie it around myself as I pad silently around the place.

When I slide back into bed, Finn stirs, and I take the chance while he's sleepy and—you'd think—vulnerable to roll and come astride him. He seems to be hard before he even opens his eyes, his hands coming to my hips. The robe slips off one shoulder as I grind softly along his erection.

Blinking up at me, Finn's lips curve. Then he grabs me, making me squeak as he pulls me down against him and rolls, putting me underneath him again.

I grunt as he pins my hands down, his knees pushing down between my legs until I'm open around him. "Not gonna let me be on top, huh?" I ask.

"Mm," he moans softly, an enticing morning sound. "No."

I open my mouth, but I'm caught off guard as his cock probes at me once, then the second time, spot on, sliding inside me. Morning-warm skin, soft in contrast to his hardness as he shifts to come deeper, Finn's voice stays low as he ducks his head down to mine. "I don't trust you," he growls and presses down, burying inside me. "So, I'm gonna keep you right where I can control you."

I'm hardly in a position to argue, so I don't.

Chapter Seven

"**S**o, this lady..."

"Amina."

"Amina, she's going to be able to tell me who wants me dead?"

Our private elevator arrives, ready to take us down so we can go straight back up to a slightly taller building where we're meeting our mysterious hostess on the rooftop. Well, mysterious to me, at least.

"She's not psychic," Finn tells me, stepping in after me. He's looking good tonight, I have to admit. As the sun goes down in an orange blaze, the temperature drops so that wearing long pants and a nice button-up is actually possible. For my part, well, we spent the afternoon browsing the shops under the hotel, the ones under the watchful eye of security. I picked out a silk dress of pale green. And given my current love life, I decided to forgo underwear. I'm getting kind of attached to the dangerous feel of going without cover, anyway.

As we walk out of the glass frontage of the hotel, two of the large men in neat black suits by the door break off and follow us. In this place, seeing people wandering around with their own security detachments is not an unusual occurrence, so I try to act like it comes naturally to me. But I can't help but glance back at them over my shoulder.

"It's only two blocks," Finn reminds me. "Try to act like this is just how you walk around."

"Followed by big men with guns?"

"Yes. Ones with your best interest at heart." He grins at me.

But I find it difficult to grin back. Finn's hand slides up to my shoulder, squeezing softly. I take a long breath and force myself to relax, letting the tension out of my shoulders.

Then we're there, in a different, large elevator. The security guards once again faded into the shadows.

The rooftop is dominated by a glimmering blue pool, separated by a white wire fence from the bar and dining areas which are dominated by circles of low couches around wide, round tables. Finn's hand on my hip directs me to the other end, where the view over the city from our dizzying height is the best.

But I shouldn't be looking at the city lights. I need to make a good impression on this woman, seeing as my life could be in her hands.

When I first see her, I'm struck by her simple elegance. A woman edging on late middle age, she holds it well; her smile lines well in-grained and endearing, her dress and shawl complimenting the deep colour of her skin. And her hair... I try not to envy the long, silky blackness of it. I could never commit to brushing my hair enough to get it to look like that.

She stands when she sees us, nodding to the small contingent of guards stationed at posts around her booth. She smiles, pulling Finn into a quick embrace, then turns to me, clasping my hand in both of hers. "You must be Elsie. Finn spoke of you."

"Did he?" I ask. Of course, he did. I'm the reason we're here. But still, the way she said it suggests something more. And indeed, from the look she shoots him, I'm sure she knows of the... *other* aspect of our relationship. I sense there's not so much of a point in hiding much from this woman.

"Sit! Come. Are you hungry?" She gestures at one of the guards. "Order us a platter, will you?"

I perch on the couch at the end of the table, and Amina retakes her place in the corner of the long lounge, Finn around from her.

"Finn told me you are a well-connected woman," I say.

"Oh, of course! It pays to be." She smiles. "Especially in your situation. It seems there's more here than first appeared."

"Yes. Someone wants me dead."

"An unfortunate circumstance."

I resist snorting. That's one way of putting it. "One I'd like to change."

Amina laughs, sitting forward to sip something from a small cup. She pours more into two other cups, and hands me one of them, pinched between her fingertips. "Come, it will relax you."

I decide to take her word for it and take a sip. I expected something akin to metho. But it's nice, nutty, even. "I just don't know why someone would be trying to kill me."

"No idea?" She peers at me. "There's no one from your life back home, someone unrelated to... all this?" 'This' seems to encapsulate whatever me and Finn have found ourselves doing.

"I mean, sure. But no one who would act on it."

She laughs again, that clear and high sound. Sitting back, crossing one knee over the other, she touches a finely manicured fingernail to her lips. "Let us consider, then. You are a private investigator. Then... Bici, is it?"

"Yes."

"They... let's call it 'convince' you to help them in rounding up poor Finn here."

Poor Finn pours himself more of the nutty alcohol.

"But that doesn't go well, for them at least. And now you are in a unique position to see inside Seahorse with the eyes of someone typically on the more conventional side of the law. And the potential to report back to them, eventually."

"This wasn't someone in Seahorse," Finn puts in.

Amina holds a finger up. "Ah, yes! I quite agree. But Seahorse, given the nature of its work, has access to other organizations, doesn't it? And perhaps someone within one of *them* would rather that Elsie here was perhaps dealt with in a more *final* way, to begin with."

Finn considers that. "So, you think it's someone Seahorse has connections to?"

Amina shrugs, taking another delicate sip. "Perhaps they worry you'll spill their secrets in the throes of some..." She smiles, and mischief glints in her dark eyes. "Emotion, or other."

Finn rolls his eyes, sitting forward. "That casts quite a wide net, Amina."

"Is there a solution to this?" I cut in.

Now her expression sobers slightly. "Until you know more about the assassin themselves, dear, you ought to stay under guard."

I sigh, falling back into my seat. "What? Forever?"

"I'm quite happy to accommodate..."

"It won't be forever. We've got lives to get on with," says Finn.

I close my lips. I feel a sinking sensation at the idea he's impatient to get rid of me. But of course I shouldn't be surprised, or hurt. This has been an intimacy of convenience. A way to pass the time.

Sensing the tension, Amina perks up. "Come, you are safe here, hm? We have the now, after all. Enjoy it! And here comes our platter."

***

I stare stubbornly ahead as the elevator takes us smoothly back up to our penthouse.

That's the problem. Thinking in *ours* and *we*. When did I start doing that? Like it's *our* room. I falter a little. There are plenty of bedrooms. How did we agree to share one? We didn't, is the answer. We just did it.

"Are you going to tell me what's wrong?" Finn asks.

I don't glance at him where he stands by my shoulder. I don't even move.

"Nothing. I'm just tired. And someone is trying to kill me."

"You're not tired. And someone was trying to kill you long before dinner."

I ignore him. The elevator doors ping open. I move to step out, only to gasp as my arm is caught. Finn spins me to face him. "Don't be difficult. What's pissing you off?"

I grit my teeth. I should have remembered his weird intuitiveness. I'm not going to get away with 'I'm tired.' Or a lie either, probably.

"What are we doing?"

He blinks down at me, clearly lost.

"Are you just waiting until I'm off your hands to get 'back on with your life'?"

Finn sighs, and I know he's remembered the words he said back on the rooftop. "That."

I click my tongue. Now I feel like a fool, making a big deal over some little words which, really, I feel the same way as he does about. I definitely feel the same way. No question about it...

Turning, I twist out of his grasp and walk into the living room, where wide windows are open to let in the evening breeze. I know he's following me, but I pretend not to know.

"I didn't mean it like that," Finn tells me, and when I don't react, just continue unbuckling my heels, he adds, somewhat exasperated, "This is no way to live."

"*This*?" Gesturing around us, at the luxury, I scoff, "You're right, it's practically a slum."

"You know what I mean."

"No, I don't. Just say what you mean."

He stares at me, mildly irritated, and something else too. "I don't want to live with your life in danger."

"Then don't. I'll make it on my own. I don't need you to babysit me."

"Again, not what I meant..."

"You kidnapped me to begin with!" I remind him, my ire building.

But I don't get much further because he crosses the space between us and kisses me. At first, I'm caught off guard.

I sink against him, his tongue sweet from the dessert bread and nutty from the wine. Then I remember that I'm angry, and I try to shove against his chest, but he presses me back against the couch, pushing deeper instead, past my resistance and anger until I'm sucked in again.

When he relents, he stays close, looking down on me, his fingers tender on my cheek.

"You're a stubborn ass."

Well, that wasn't what I was expecting. I open my mouth, but he goes on. "I don't want you to go back to your life. Any more than I want to go back to mine. I want one together. But just not where you might be taken away from me at any moment."

"Oh." I should say more, but I've never been good at admitting feelings. As this whole argument probably demonstrates. I feel my stomach flutter. "I... didn't, uh..."

"You don't have to commit right now," he says, smiling. I stop stammering. Ducking down, Finn slides an arm behind my knees, scooping me into his arms to carry me toward the bedroom. "Let's carry on in a language you're fluent in, huh?" Finn muses, setting my feet down beside the bed.

Now that, I can get behind. I push him back on the bed and move over him as he shimmies further back, pulling his shirt open all the way down as I do. Settling over his hips, I shrug out of my straps, flipping the top of my dress down to expose my breasts, which his hands close on like magnets.

Grinning, I lean over and kiss him, grinding down on the quickly growing bulge in the front of his pants.

"You really want to be on top, huh?" Finn props up on his elbows, catching my lips.

"Mm-hm. I'll behave..." My voice dips, suggesting the opposite. "I promise."

"Alright," he concedes. But before I can relish in victory, he grips my thighs, lifting me up a little on my knees.

I frown. "What are you..." My voice cuts off as he wriggles downwards, quickly putting his shoulders under my hips, then his head between my legs. "Oh."

His mouth traces warm up the inside of my thigh, hands still gripping me, pulling me down onto his face. Propped up on my fists, I lull a little, already dizzy with anticipation as his tongue traces higher, under my rolled-up dress, to where I'm exposed for lack of underwear. "Fuck," I breathe.

Mumbling a laugh, Finn flicks his tongue over me, a first touch that has me panting. Then his mouth closes over me, his hands pulling me down firmer so that he covers me. I gasp, then bite my lip.

I really ought to drag this out. It's worth extending. But I doubt my ability to control myself to that extent. Seeming to sense this, Finn slows down, stroking near but not on my clit, dragging it out for me whether I have the self-restraint to do it myself or not. "Oh my god," I gasp. "Jesus."

My hips move on him, small movements which I try to restrain but soon lose even that. I feel too sensitive, the build-up so intense it's almost painful. I try to lift away, to lessen it, but his arms loop over my thighs from the back, his mouth latched around me, suddenly teasing my most sensitive part until I'm a panting mess.

At last, I feel myself cross the point of no return, and I cry out, leaning into my fists, spasming as he holds me in place. The absolute pleasure crashes through me, and it's all I can do to stay vaguely upright. He moans against me, bracing me through the orgasm, and as the peak passes, he loosens, letting me lift away from the sensations which are now too much, almost tickling.

I blink my eyes open. That was...

Finn is sliding out from under me. Suddenly, he's behind me instead, and with me on all fours, I'm all for him taking advantage of that positioning. Leaning over my back, he murmurs, "Your boobs looked great from down there." His hand slides up my ribs, then underneath me to cup me. "And from up here. From everywhere, really."

I giggle, still a little dizzy. That passes quickly, however, as I feel his knees settle between mine, his cock pressing where I'm wet and as ready as I've ever been. He slides inside me slowly, filling me, and I moan, long and low, with it. My lingering sensitivity lends to belated aftershocks, and I don't know if anything has ever felt so good.

It has, I'm sure, but right now I'm biased.

Weighing against me, Finn presses me almost flat onto the bed, one hand still cupping my breast, his hips thrusting long and slow against me, making both of us groan each time he pushes deep again. I squeeze, pressing back on him and tightening.

"Mm, this is not going to go for very long if you keep doing that," Finn warns, breath sliding over the back of my neck.

"No?" I ask, arching my back a little more, pulling him a little deeper.

He mutters a curse, thrusting deeper and holding. I can feel his breath quicken in the way his torso expands against my back.

But moving back against him the way I have been has been stroking me as much as him, and amazingly, despite the powerful orgasm that just racked me, I suddenly feel that I'm on the edge of another one. So even as Finn holds still to gain control, I can't help but wriggle back against him, arching to grate backwards until I'm gasping.

I feel the moment he realizes that I'm about to spasm around him again because he curses and weighs heavier on me, his hand tangling in my hair.

I cry out as he thrusts hard and fast into me, riding out my climax with his own, his pleasure mingling with mine as his hand tightens in my hair and he grunts, breath heavy, until he finally loses his control and his rhythm.

For a time, he lies collapsed along my back. I close my eyes, and possibly even drift off for a moment. But in the end, the heat lifts him off me, and I roll over to lay my hand on his bare chest. I'd forgotten I was still wearing my dress, if only as a scrunched belt around my waist, and he his pants, though barely.

"That," I say, "still doesn't count as me being on top."

***

An hour after dawn the next day, we're in the back of a car with no glass in the windows and a suspension I would best describe as *rickety*.

"How far is it?" I ask after what feels like the tenth close call on a narrow street between otherwise large buildings.

"An hour, maybe," Finn tells me. He's wearing a loose, white long-sleeve and beige pants. The heat is oppressive. Room service brought me pale, ultra-wide-legged pants and a burnt orange ankle-length cardigan as well as a matching headscarf, telling me in no uncertain terms that I would either burn or faint if I went out in what I'd already had on. I took their word for it, but there's no air conditioning in the cab except for what hot air blasts in through the windows, so I'm still sweating inside my lightweight clothes.

The car rumbles down a bare road for some time, and I stare at the emptiness of the desert rolling away to each side, and I forget how flattened the seat cushion is, how the air conditioning doesn't work, how the radio cuts in and out frequently.

I've never seen such an expanse of harsh landscape, seeming to stretch on forever before it fades into a distant mirage. Eventually, the flatness recedes, and small dotted villages start appearing. At one, the cab pulls off and drops us among homes patched together with galvanized iron and wood scraps.

I stand on the side of the road, which bears little distinction from the road itself, and feel overdressed in my expensive clothes. Finn is at my arm, leading me. The people stare but not unduly, and I guess it mustn't be too uncommon for city people to happen by. For what, I'd rather not imagine.

A few houses down, at one made of misaligned mud bricks, a man is waiting outside, wringing his hands. His face is warm but tense, and when he sees us, he breaks into a nervous smile, gesturing us inside in his own language, which I, of course, don't speak.

Inside, the house is one room and deceptively cool. A woman sits on a cushion on the floor, a baby quiet in her arms. Two more children stare at us wide-eyed from the darker edges of the room. They wave for us to take a seat on the cushions laid over the floor of hard-packed dirt, and the man takes a seat also, pouring us tea while his wife nods and smiles at us.

I'm disarmed by how warm and healthy these people look. Their clothes have seen better days, bearing signs of repair and the bleached remnants of stains, but their eyes are bright and hopeful.

Once we've been poured tea, the man gestures at the larger of the two children, a girl, and she approaches cautiously until he pulls her to a seat on his knee. Then he speaks, and as the girl repeats, I realise with shock that she is going to be our translator. Her clear, small and heavily accented voice relays to us: "We have discussed at length. And we would like to go further with your offer. My wife is no longer safe here. Her pregnancy was some protection, but now she has given birth, and the city man will be less likely to stay away. We need to leave soon."

I glance between Finn and the others. What is going on? These people surely can't afford Seahorse's services.

Finn nods and smiles at the girl. "Tell your dad I'm glad. We'll take care of you and your family." He reaches into a satchel bag he's brought and pulls out a handful of papers and passports. "The day after tomorrow, a car much like the cab we came in will come and retrieve all of you. You must act like it is merely an outing, and that you plan to be back. This is very important. The car will take you to the airport." He hands the girl the papers. "These state your right to emigrate to my country. My friends will keep you in their safe house for a time. It will not be so comfortable, but you will learn some more

English and be put in jobs. Once you are established, you will make your own way in your new home."

I can only watch silently as the meeting proceeds. When the passport with her face on it is passed to the woman, she blinks, her eyes glassy and nods in thanks.

I realise now that Seahorse really is not what I thought. And perhaps not what Bici thinks either.

***

In the car on the way back, we're silent for a time. Finally, I glance over at Finn, where he stares pensively out at the dry country we pass through. "It's charity. Isn't it? You're not sending them to work in factories or something?"

Finn laughs softly, meeting my eye. "No, we're not sending them to work in factories."

I nod. "Why did they need to leave?"

Sighing heavily, Finn tells me, "Mira, the wife. She'd caught the eye of some oil tycoon or other. He keeps coming to the village, and well, men like that are not so great at taking no for an answer."

"That's awful."

"Well, she was safe while she was pregnant. But something like that could destroy their family. A man can't raise children alone here. If she were taken away, he could lose his son, his two daughters as well. They'd end up in a textile factory, or worse. So, they need to leave. Somewhere they can't be found."

"And that's where you come in."

"Yeah."

"Is that what you did for Amina?"

Finn nods slowly, a distant look in his eye. "Amina was in a village like that, yes. She was the village medicine woman. Married. Her husband was older, a lot older, and a grumpy bastard as far as I could tell. Amina had only given him one child, a girl, Taif. Something her husband never quite appreciated. Then he started talking about selling Taif. That she was no use to them at home." Finn meets my eye. "Taif was eight."

I pull a face. "God."

"So, Amina started looking for help. But she didn't want to leave her country. So, we did the best we could, and set her and her daughter up in Dubai with a security guard in case her husband came knocking. A couple of years later, the husband is dead of natural causes, and Amina has started a business. Paradise Skin. And, well, you know how the rest goes. She was very successful."

"Happily ever after, huh?"

"Something like that."

"So why does she spend her money on penthouses and special cars? Why not put it all through you guys?"

Finn shakes his head. "You know how when someone wins the lottery or comes into money in a shady way, they shouldn't go and remodel their kitchen and buy a Lambo and the like?"

"Yeah."

"Well, Amina has the opposite problem. Everyone knows her skincare made it big. Celebrities endorse it for pity's sake, and it doesn't go cheap. So she could live in a three-bed house in the suburbs and drive herself places. But that's not how someone does it here. It would attract attention."

"Right. Seahorse isn't exactly a tax write-off kind of charity."

"No. We operate somewhat below board."

I frown. "Where are we going?"

"Amina texted me. She said to meet her at an underground restaurant near here. She might have information for us."

I shift. Think of the assassin again.

Finn squeezes my hand. "Hey, it'll be okay. Amina has the place locked down."

I manage a smile back.

***

The restaurant is quite literally underground, under a skyscraper.

The lights are orange, leaning towards red, and the place seems to have been emptied for Amina and her detail. Her daughter is there too, and she introduces Taif, now fourteen. The girl beams at us, and something about her presence is reassuring to me.

As we sit down and order food, Amina taps Taif on the hip. "Go with Andrea and do your homework, darling."

Like the best-behaved teenager I've ever seen, Taif waves shyly at us and slides out of her side of the booth, disappearing with five guards of her own towards the back of the restaurant. Then Amina shifts and faces us. "I've got news about your... issue."

I feel my heart rate pick up. I'm sitting close enough beside Finn to feel his leg brushing mine under the table, but I have the sudden urge to be even closer.

She looks to Finn. "Are you familiar with Owl?"

Finn's hesitation is not reassuring to me. Then he nods slowly. "It's them?"

"I'm almost certain."

A frown appears between his brows. I'm looking between both of them. "Is that bad? Who's Owl?"

Finn takes a deep breath. "Owl is an organization. Of contract killers. Very efficient. Very highly paid."

"Oh," is all I can say.

Amina adds, "Which means someone with means is behind this. And they're not likely to stop."

I feel a little dizzy again. Not fainting dizzy but sort of out-of-body dizzy. "I see. So they won't stop."

Amina opens her mouth. But Finn speaks. "We'll stop them." But I see their expressions. It's dire, even if they're not telling me. Perhaps I'm as good as dead.

"Any idea why?" Finn asks Amina.

She shrugs. "Wrong person, wrong place. Someone is nervous about an insider with Bici being in their world."

"But I'm not an insider at Bici!" I put in, as though arguing my case with Amina will make a difference. "They basically blackmailed me."

"It doesn't appear to matter to them, dear."

I blink, then nod. Turning to Finn, I ask, even though I already know, "Everyone near me is in danger, aren't they? If they're this serious."

"Elsie..."

"It's true."

"It doesn't matter. I'll handle it."

Brows drawing together, I ask, because I truly don't understand, "Why?"

Finn's mouth opens, but he can't explain it either. Why would he risk his life for me?

I shake my head, standing up. "Excuse me. I need to use the bathroom."

"Elsie..."

"I'm fine. I just need a minute," I call back, already on my way to the softly glowing pink sign at the back of the venue.

***

Taif is washing her hands when I come in, her book tucked under her arm. "Sorry," I mutter, my mind elsewhere.

"It's okay," she says, catching my eye. "Mum says you're far from home. Will you live here now?"

I open my mouth, caught off guard. "I don't know."

"We were running away too once. But it all worked out in the end. It will for you too."

That brings a smile to my face. "Thanks, Taif."

After she all but skips from the room, I sit and hold my head in my hands in a cubicle. The floor is black marble.

I need to be honest with myself. Why not start now, when I might die today, after all? And the honest truth is I want the life Finn spoke about. Together, doing god knows what, but who cares? I want the morning sex and the closeness, and the simple desire to be in each other's company.

But, and it's a big *but*, I know I can't. I can't take what he offers, knowing I'd be risking these people. Not just him. Amina, Taif, all of Seahorse.

It doesn't take me long to reach a decision. I just can't, not where there is such a high chance that someone besides me will be hurt instead. I've done some questionable things in my life, but I won't let Taif or Finn be caught in the crossfire just by virtue of being in the way at the wrong moment.

I lift my head. There's a window, narrow and high up, but level with the ground outside.

It'll have to do.

Chapter Eight

This could be a bad decision. But what decision can I make at the moment that won't be a poor one? I have nothing, just my tiny handbag slung across my body on a long strap—better to fend off pickpockets—and a few notes that aren't even appropriate for this country. And my phone. Finn gave it back to me last night. I didn't even know he had it; I'd thought it lost back on that first fateful night.

It was a gesture of trust, giving it to me. One I'm now punishing.

I drift along with a scant crowd, sticking to the shady side of the street like most of the people game enough to even be out in the afternoon here. My heart pounds. Finn will twig on soon. He'll look for me, then realise I ran away after all. Without me, he will have less protection from Bici. But I saw his face. I know Owl is worse than Bici could ever be.

Soon the buildings get a smidge shorter, and following the shade brings me under the cover of a marketplace. Giant triangular shade cloths in varying colours are strung between the buildings to cast the stalls beneath in shade.

Currency. That's a good first order of business, I decide.

The market is huge. Busy even during this, the hottest time of the day. People brush past me; children run and shout. I tell myself that I'm safe in such a public place, but I can't shake the feeling of eyes on me, of someone watching. I walk through the fresh produce tables, avoiding the peddlers and people standing at corners and pedestrian intersections holding pamphlets. I don't know any of their language to express 'not interested.'

Once I make it out to a brief alley of sunlight between the shades, I see the building. It's small, squat and made of stone, with opaque glass and varying kinds of currency icons over the steps. Exactly what I'm looking for.

I don't know if I get a good deal. Probably not. But money from home is hardly going to do me much good here. I make sure to stash it in my satchel bag before I step out of the cool interior of the currency exchange.

A peddler I didn't notice on my way in is waiting at the bottom of the three steps. He's holding roses, his face obscured by his loose, black head wrapping.

"No thank you," I try to say as I move to duck past him. But he doesn't understand, and he sidesteps to stay in my way, pushing the roses toward me again. I turn and go to step around him the other way, toward the side of the building where large bins attract flies in the hot air. The peddler steps forward, and suddenly, I'm cornered against the bins.

It strikes me with what feels like an electric shock through my heart that where I am right now would be the easiest place to leave a body, a place people might not immediately notice. At the same time, I see something glint in the roses. Long and thin and metal. A syringe.

I go to scream, but his hand is over my mouth. Lashing out, I manage to dodge the jab of that syringe and whatever fatal concoction might be inside. But my back has come up against the largest of the bins. There's nowhere else to go.

Suddenly, my attacker jerks back, and then like magic, or all my wishes coming true, he is dragged away from me. A huge figure has him by the back of the neck. The assassin tries to spin, to lunge at this new person, but there's a quick strike—I hear it more than see it—and he slumps, falling limp and heavy to the ground.

Heart pounding, I look from their unconscious but breathing form to my rescuer.

"*Agent Theo*?!"

He grabs me by the arm. "Are you hurt? Did he inject you?"

"I..." Oh god, did he? Am I any minute now going to breathe my last breath? As blackness creeps in at the edge of my vision, I realise I'm not breathing. I force a breath, closing my eyes. No. I feel normal. Shaken and full of adrenaline, but normal. I open my eyes, my vision returning to normal. Theo is staring at me. "No. I'm okay."

Theo glances around. The only things stopping a crowd from gathering are the bins blocking the view from one side, and, at least in part, Theo's stature. He pulls the deep red scarf from around his shoulders, which, in other circumstances, I'd have pointed out to him was *not* helping him blend in, and rolls the limp body over toward the bins before throwing the scarf over him. "He'll be out for an hour or so. Why was he attacking you? Is he part of Seahorse? Have you escaped Finn?"

"I... what? No." I shake my head. How did Theo find me? How did the assassin find me? It's got to be the same answer for both. There's no other explanation.

I back away from Theo. When he notices, he frowns at me and takes a step toward me, which only makes me back up faster.

Theo holds his hands up, stopping where he is. "Elsie. I'm here to take you home. *Safely*."

I'm shaking my head. "How?"

"How?" His forehead creases.

"How did you find me?" I point at the figure under the scarf. "How did *he*?"

A muscle in Theo's jaw twitches, then he says, "I found you through the tracker."

I blink. "Tracker..."

"I didn't agree with it. Back in the van, when they... when I took your DNA sample. It was an insertion too. I thought we should have told you. But I couldn't have found you without it."

My mouth has come open. I can't believe it. But I can. My finger goes to the back of my scalp. To the weird lump of scar tissue that wasn't healing right. All this time...

"*You* couldn't have found me without it? Neither could he!" I shout. I can't believe this. All this time, that's how the assassin was finding me. That's what's been risking my life, what's almost killed me twice now. I want to scratch it right out of my head.

Theo frowns. He doesn't get it. Or he's pretending not to. Either way, I keep my distance. "The man trying to kill me is with Owl. And you have the tracker on me to tell them where to find me. You used it yourself!"

Theo spreads his hands. "Elsie, I'm not trying to kill you. I'm trying to get you out of this mess. You should never have been in it in the first place. If it's really Owl... we can fix it. We can protect you."

I laugh because it's either that or cry. "Don't you get it? If it's not you who put the hit on me, then it's someone else at Bici. Either way, I can't go back there."

Theo blinks. I see it dawning on him, and I really want to believe it wasn't him. That I wasn't set up to fail from the start, with some kind of screwed kill-switch built in. But I'm too frazzled. No, I can't take the chance. I've backed out into the open. Glancing around, I know

I need to get away, get a knife to this thing behind my ear before they can send out the next hitman. Theo can see that I'm about to make a move. "Elsie, just stay calm..."

"I'm sorry."

"Don't—"

"Help!" I scream at the top of my lungs. "Help! He's trying to kidnap me!" People are looking up; some are being drawn over. "Help!" I scream again. Now they start running over, attention on Theo, the big, scary-looking, clearly foreign guy in their market.

I see Theo curse, looking around at the hostile crowd. But that's all I see because I turn and slip away, casting off the cardigan and scarf as I go. The nearby stalls have emptied at the commotion, and I grab a pale blue wrapping on my way past, throwing it over my shoulders. Hopefully, I can be forgiven for this one petty theft, given the circumstances.

I glance back toward where Theo is lost in the crowd. A security guard runs past me, and I keep my head down and keep walking. I hope Theo can manage to grab my would-be assassin, but I think there's not so much chance of that with the commotion I've caused. I turn a corner, heading for the street, and run straight into someone solid.

In my state, I squeak and leap backwards. Hands grab me by the shoulders, and I struggle in panic. Another assassin, it must be. What will it be this time? A knife? A gun? I look up into his face... and almost faint with relief.

Finn is staring down at me with wide eyes, his brow creased in concern. He pulls me against him. "Thank god. I was looking for you; I heard the commotion." There's a lightness in Finn's voice as he adds, "Thought you must have something to do with it." But I can hear the strain in his words, how worried he was.

I clutch him tight for a beat. My eyes prick, and I tell myself now is not the time to burst into tears. Save it for later. Pushing back, in a rush to explain, I manage to get out, "Finn. There's a tracker. In my head. I didn't know."

"A tracker... What?"

"Just..." I slice my hands through the air. "How doesn't matter. Getting it out does."

"Shit. Okay. Come on."

***

"This might hurt. You sure you don't want anesthetic?"

Given the state of the bathroom we're in, and the smell of the toilet I'm perched on, even with its lid closed, I think *antiseptic* is more in order. I have a towel over my shoulders, my hair tipped forward like I'm about to have my hair dyed in a college dorm. This is not far off, being the first hotel we came across, and the receptionist offered for us to pay by the hour.

We agreed to anything, but probably not for the reasons she thought.

"Like hell am I going to wait here for a guy with a noose while you go and scrounge for numbing cream. Just get the damned thing out and flush it!"

"Have it your way."

The sting is sharp. I grit my teeth and grip the corners of the towel against my chest. I feel a scrape, my skin tugging as he drags the knife. I remind myself the incision can't be more than a centimeter. So the images running through my head of long gashes in my scalp and bald patches are just unrealistic. But that doesn't help so much.

"Okay. I see it. Just getting it…"

"Mother of fuck," I hiss as the sting spreads and turns to a blunt throb.

"…out. Aha! There we go!" The pressure lets up. I feel a slight trickle on the back of my neck. Finn tears something open, a tissue packet, then I feel him pressing one to the back of my neck. "Hold here."

I press the tissue to my neck and sit up slowly. The pain diminishes, helped by a rush of relief as I look up and see the tiny, green cylindrical chip Finn is holding between his finger and thumb while he stands in front of me.

"What are you waiting for? Throw it in the sink, feed it to a pigeon, get rid of it!"

Finn is staring at it, though. "We could do that. Or…"

"Or?"

Meeting my eye, he asks, "The assassin thinks you're alone, right? They'll try again as soon as they can?"

"I guess so…" I say. Like many times before with him, something tells me I won't like where his mind is going.

***

The room smells, somehow, even worse at night. But that's not the worst thing about it. As I attempt such stillness that I'm hardly even breathing, squatting in the closet, watching through the gap between the cupboard door, the worst thing is that the hotel room door is ever so softly clicking. Just like that night in the woods house. And just like then, it creeps open.

My heart hammers as I spy the dark figure. He turns to the bed and the figure lying there, my tracker beneath. *Come on Finn,* I think, *you'd better know what you're doing.*

The footsteps are soft, barely audible, as he steps up to the bed. I see his hand raise. A gun, this time. This guy sure likes variety. A single shot, silenced but still loud in the quiet room. Then stillness. More silence. I feel like my heartbeat is too loud.

Then the lights come on. Finn steps out of the bathroom, gun trained on the assassin, as do three other men, courtesy of Amina.

"Drop it."

The assassin glances at the bed, flicks back the quilt to reveal naught but a pillow with a hole in the middle. It's an old trick, but hey, it works. His cruel line of mouth twists a little in a smirk.

"I said drop it."

He does. One of the men ducks forward, pocketing the pistol.

"Frisk him," Finn instructs.

As they do, they pull out an array of other weapons, which make me a little nauseous to watch as they're deposited on the bed. Capsules, more syringes, garroting cords.

A gallery of the ways I might have died.

"Okay, you can come out now," Finn calls.

Taking a deep breath, I step out of the closet. The assassin turns to me. His eyes are small and pale. He would have enjoyed it, I see then, and I feel no remorse for the prison he'll spend the rest of his life in.

"Get his phone too," I say. "I want to see who he's been talking to."

"Is this the same man as at the market?" Finn asks.

"Yes," I answer.

Nodding, Finn lowers his gun because the other three men still have theirs trained on the hitman, and one of them cuffs his hands behind his back.

Finn steps over to me. I've pulled my phone out of my pocket. His hand comes to mine, over the screen, so that I have to look up and meet his eyes. "You sure he's not the one that ordered it?"

"You know him. Do you think it is?" I ask.

Finn nods softly, his hand sliding away.

In truth, I have no way of being sure, but I've ignored my gut before, and I'm not going to do it again.

So, I call Theo.

He can come and get Bici's assassin for them.

Afterwards, I drop the phone in the toilet.

"Come on." Finn's hand holds my elbow. "If I know Theo, he won't be long."

The hot, tepid air outside, as we duck under a shade cloth bolted to the side of the building, feels like the most refreshing, sweet air I've ever tasted. I gasp at it, my head spinning, arms moving dream-like in front of me as I reach to stabilize myself. By the time I realise I'm dizzy, coming down from adrenaline and fear and all the other things that come with thinking you're going to die, Finn already has me propped against the cool cement wall.

"It's okay," he murmurs against my hair, arms around me, holding me upright as I rest my head heavily on his shoulder. My eyes are open, but all I can see are yellow blotches. It's not unpleasant, though it should be. I feel safe. I know Finn will stay here with me, and I slump against him. "Just breathe with me." His voice comes to me like an echo.

When his chest expands against mine, steady and slow, I do as he says, following his exhale, then breathing deep together, so our bodies press ever firmer. My vision clears a little more with each long breath. I manage to lift my head, the episode passing, leaving me weak but somehow light.

Letting my head rest back against the wall, I look at Finn's face. He smiles at me, a counter to the line of worry between his brows and the concern in his eyes as he watches me.

Managing a wry laugh, I comment, "You know, one of these days we're going to have to actually get to know each other."

He breathes a laugh. "Well, I like yellow. And I like peaches. They're my favorite food."

"Hm," I consider, testing whether my hands work as I rest them on his arms, which are still looped around my waist. I'm not totally sure I could stand on my own yet. "I like red. And broccoli."

Finn pulls a face. "*Broccoli*? Well, that's a deal-breaker."

"Oh, no." I break out into a laugh, and Finn grins as he nuzzles my cheek with his nose.

"Feeling okay?"

"I don't know about okay... but I do need a drink."

***

I force Finn to follow me to the nearest and loudest bar, which, naturally, is a tourist trap. But it's loud and dark, and the floor is sticky, and I decide it's just what I need.

"Well done. You've managed to find the biggest dive in Dubai," Finn muses, nursing his first drink while I'm already on my second.

I ignore him, pulling him onto the dance floor where we're so mushed together that dancing is kind of an afterthought.

Somehow, at some stage, we stumble back into the relative spaciness of the bar. I've just done another shot when Finn takes up my peripherals, which are slightly blurrier than the rest of my vision, shouting to be heard over the blaring music. "I hate to ruin your party. But once

Owl discovers their hitman is down, they'll send another. We should be somewhere..." He glances around. A man in a hot pink speedo has started dancing on the bar. *Tourists.* "...quieter."

I throw my arms around him and kiss him instead. Sloppily, I have to admit. "So? How are they going to find me?" I throw my hands in the air and do a spin.

"They wouldn't be very good hitmen if they all relied on trackers in their targets' heads," he says, managing to sound wry, even while shouting.

I do a little wiggle. "Who cares! I'm alive!"

Finn's hand closes around the new shot that I'm lifting toward my face, which appeared from somewhere obscure. "How about we slow down on those, huh?"

"Gahhhh!" I stick my tongue out. "You're such a *goody* for a criminal."

"Why don't you say that a little louder?"

Ignoring him again, I link my arms around the back of his neck and grin up at him like a besotted schoolgirl. "Did you mean it?"

Finn tilts his head. "No, I don't really want you to say that I'm a criminal even louder."

I click my tongue, lightly hitting him on the shoulder. "Don't tease me. You know I'm talking about what you said before. About being together," I add, extending the word *being* out so that it packs at least two more syllables.

The corner of his mouth twitches. "Yes. I meant it."

"Really?"

"You are the one that ran away today, you know," he points out.

I roll my eyes, stepping back. I'm not in the mood for logic. I go to pull him back toward the dance floor, but Finn hugs me to him again, voice dipping low. "Why don't I take you home, huh? I'll run you a nice bubble bath, bring you some champagne…"

"Ooh!" I smile. He knows how to speak my language. "Will you be in the bath?"

"Of course!" he promises with an enthusiasm that, if I were sober, I'd be able to pick out as fake. The poor guy just wants some peace and quiet with me safely in bed.

***

Unfortunately for me, but perhaps fortunately for Finn, I pass out in the cab back to the hotel, so I never get my bubble bath.

But I do get my hangover, and then some. The happy morning sun, and Finn's somewhat smug face, wakes me up. I groan and roll back over, burying my head under the pillow.

"Come on. I've got orange juice, coffee, tea… Pick your poison."

I groan and sit up. The world spins a smidge. Finn sets down a heavily laden breakfast tray on a little arched table designed for eating in bed. It does smell good…

"Start with the coffee," I croak.

Eventually, I graduate to toast, and then I feel somewhat better. Almost human, even.

"Good night?" Finn asks.

I don't appreciate the way he grins while he asks it. "Divine. Thank you."

"Hey, you needed to let loose a little, right?"

"Mmmm." Then I fix my gaze on him. "You owe me a bubble bath."

"And champagne?"

I groan. Finn laughs. Reaching into his pocket, he pulls out a phone. It takes me a moment to realise it's the assassins. "Ready to look yet?"

I nod slowly. "Ready as I'll ever be."

Finn shifts until he's beside me, and I watch as he turns the phone back on.

The contact list is short. A burner phone, then. They all have one-letter names. A. G. J. When Finn taps on a name, the number it's attached to makes no sense. Full of hyphens and dashes. "Encrypted." Finn shakes his head. "No way to decipher it from this. The only way to tell who these numbers belong to would be to be in the same room with someone when their phone rings."

I sigh. "Right, of course."

We're quiet for a moment, coming to conclusions. I meet his eye. "You know I have to leave again."

Nodding, eyes downcast, Finn says, "I know."

"I'll come back on my own this time."

Finn squeezes my hand. "I know."

Chapter Nine

They don't know the name on the fake passport acquired for me by Finn, or at least I have to assume they don't, and I return home, without issue and alone.

I don't go to my apartment first. Why would I? They'll be there, waiting to bring me in. And I'm too busy bringing myself in to go through with all of that.

With nothing but the clothes on my back and a small satchel bag taken up mostly by my fake IDs, I walk right into the building and catch the lift straight up to Bici. It's surprisingly easy.

The headquarters floor is somewhat less impressive than I'd imagined. Big and sprawling, yes, but really it could be the offices of any law enforcement agency, complete with divider cubicles separating about two dozen deceptively normal-looking employees. The carpet is worn in places, and the place feels somewhat grey.

Nonetheless, when I stand in the doorway in full view, faces look up from their computers and stare. I imagine they've seen my face in some company-wide memo, but they're just trying to reason how likely it is that a person a handful of their best are out looking for has just walked right into their office.

Very likely, as it turns out.

A small, pretty woman in clothes that don't flatter her at all stands cautiously up from her desk and approaches me. I read her name tag. *Nina.*

You should get out of here, Nina. This place will use you up too, I want to warn her.

"Elsie Burke?" she checks.

"That's me."

"Oh." She blinks, bites her lip. "Ah, come right this way…"

They have their own holding cells here. Cute. Nina seems caught off guard by being the one to lead someone to them, and a willing person at that. Though she doesn't look too capable of manhandling me if it comes to it.

As I sit in a room much like the first holding cell I was in, what feels like a lifetime ago, in an identical metal chair, she lingers by the door. "Can I, uh, get you a coffee?"

I smile at her. "Is Theo in?"

"I think he's been called."

"Do me a favor. Make sure he knows I'm here before anyone else does."

***

Theo looks, unsurprisingly, shocked to see me as he steps into the interrogation room. He also looks somewhat angry. I wonder how it went with the mob I set on him back in Dubai.

He sits down across from me without saying anything.

"Did you get the assassin I sent you?"

"Mm-hm," he rumbles.

"I'm guessing he didn't say anything."

"No," he admits, then leans forward on his elbows. "You had a mission. Where is Finn?"

I shouldn't press, but I ask because I need to know, "You never mentioned that you grew up with Finn."

"That wasn't relevant to your mission. It still isn't," Theo answers, lifting his chin. But there was the slightest hesitation, a slight darkening to his expression.

I hold his eye. "Do you really believe what you say about him? Do you really hate him?"

Theo stands suddenly, turning to leave.

"Wait," I say quickly. He turns back, thank god, because I need him here if my half-cocked plan is going to work. I raise my hands a little way. "Fine. I won't ask anything more about it."

He stays hovering behind his chair. "Where is he?"

"Come on," I say, meeting his eye. "We both know that's not what's keeping you up at night anymore. You want to know who in Bici is buddy enough with Owl to ask them to send a hitman after me."

I see the muscle in his jaw twitch. He says nothing. Neither do I. Eventually, he gives in first. "I assume you have some kind of proposal on how to give me that."

I grin. "I sure do." He doesn't look impressed yet, but I'm used to that from him. "You have the things I was brought in with? The phone?"

"Yes."

"Get it."

"If this is some kind of game..."

I roll my eyes. "Humor me, would you?"

I get the feeling he doesn't do that often. Without a word, Theo stands and leaves the room.

If this doesn't go the way I'm expecting... I'm screwed.

The door opens again. But it's not Theo.

"Melvin," I say. "It's been too long."

He sighs like I've disappointed him somehow, like he expected better. "It appears you have failed the mission parameters, Ms. Burke."

"Oh, I don't think *that'll* be a problem for too much longer."

He frowns at me, but Theo chooses that moment to come back in, a small zip lock bag with the assassin's phone in his hand.

"Agent Theo, why are you bringing this woman what she asks for? She ought to be in a jumpsuit by now. She went directly against our orders!"

"There may still be useful information she can give us," Theo tells him, then faces me before Melvin can argue with him. "I've got it. What do you want with it?"

"This is the phone I got off the assassin before I handed him over to you in Dubai. Turn it on." He does. "Now go to the contacts."

"Agent Theo, I really must protest. We don't know where this device comes from. If it's even really what she says… Bringing her in on this was a mistake."

"And call him," I say, glancing straight toward Melvin. Theo's brow draws down. There's silence as we all come to terms with what I've just implied.

"You can't be suggesting…" Melvin laughs, then realizes Theo isn't outright dismissing it. "She's baiting you!"

But Theo is still holding my eye. He's considering it. Melvin presses again. He seems to be growing more tense by the moment. So, I'm right? I've got to be right… "Agent Theo, go and bring Albert. That's an order."

Theo blinks. I sit forward. "If you leave me alone in this room with him, I guarantee I'll end up dead before you come back. The cameras will have a glitch. He'll say I went mad and attacked him. He has no choice."

Melvin scoffs, but at this point, neither of us is paying him mind. The phone is still in Theo's giant hand, waiting. He glances down at it. "Which number?"

I contain my sigh of relief. He's going to do it. This may work out yet.

"There's only five. Call all of them."

He taps the first one. It rings out.

"Agent Theo, if you continue to disobey direct orders, I'm going to have to—"

It happens so suddenly, I barely understand it, but afterwards, Theo has his knee in Melvin's back, the smaller man face-down where the stone floor meets the wall. Melvin's arm is twisted up behind his back, and he flops around sort of like a fish, his glasses askew. It would be gratifying if my own situation wasn't quite so dire.

Theo, the phone still in his other hand, ignores Melvin's threats to do things like *report him* and dials the second number. It rings out.

Then the third. I start to sweat.

The fourth. Theo meets my eye. If I've just made him assault his colleague for nothing...

Ringing. We both look towards the sound. Towards where it comes from, inside Melvin's hip pocket. Even Melvin has suddenly fallen quiet.

The door bursts open. As many officers as will fit in the room, and Albert, the head of Bici whom I had the pleasure of meeting once before during my recruitment, bursts in. Half a dozen guns hover somewhere between me and Theo, unsure who to point at. Theo pulls the ringing phone out of Melvin's pocket and checks it against the phone he's calling from, ignoring everything else.

Albert blinks. "What is that?"

"This is the phone of an assassin who was trying to kill Ms. Burke. And this..." Theo leans heavier into his knee, where it jabs into Melvin's back. "Is the one who sent that assassin."

Albert is staring at Melvin. I stay very still. I hardly need some trigger-happy new guy to squeeze a little too hard.

Finally, Albert asks, "You're sure?"

Theo only nods, jaw tight.

Nodding, Albert runs a hand over his forehead, his balding scalp. Then he seems to remember all the weapons in the room. He gestures, and the guns lower. I let out a breath I didn't know I was holding. "Arrest him," Albert orders, and Theo stands, taking a step back as two other officers haul Melvin to his feet and toward the door. Before he disappears, Theo speaks up, and he can only be talking to Melvin. "Why?"

Melvin, his face still a little purple from bearing Theo's weight, a vein sticking out in his temple, manages a smirk. "If you don't understand now, Agent Gertin, you never will."

Theo frowns. What does that even mean? But Albert orders him to be dragged off before the words can turn ugly. When Theo comes over to me, I'm surprised when the first thing he does is uncuff me. I stand, stepping back, waiting.

Albert watches but says nothing, though I can tell by the set of his mouth that he's displeased. One of his officers was just found to have close ties with a very criminal organisation, so I suppose if I were him, I wouldn't be looking too happy either.

"Am I free to go?" I ask.

"We have some questions..."

"No," Theo cuts him off. When Albert's surprised expression turns on him, he says firmly, "You know I disliked involving a civilian from the start, especially with what we were asking her to do. She should never have been involved, and if you continue to insist, I'll hand in my badge."

"Theodore..." Albert tries to reason.

"I was a part of this under protest. I told you. When we discussed the tracker, I was strongly against it. I won't be pushed any further on this case. It was wrong from the start."

I keep my mouth shut. I almost feel bad for entertaining the idea that Theo was involved. Albert wavers. And I can hardly blame him. Theo's gaze would make me back slowly out of the room, too.

"Very well." Albert looks at me. "You are free to go."

"And what about Finn?"

Albert frowns. "Mr. Damron is here?"

"No. I want you to drop your case on him. You've got bigger things to worry about."

"Miss Burke, I don't think you're in a position..."

"Listen," I say. "I don't want this to come across like blackmail, *but* I'm more than happy to take my story about how I was strong-armed by a national agency to the press." I let my words hang before I add, "If you keep pursuing Finn Damron."

Silence. Albert has lost his mediative tone. "I'd recommend you take your business far away from here on, Miss Burke. Damron too."

"Oh, don't worry. We're going to be very far out of your way," I promise. Turning to Theo, I meet his eye. "Thanks. But you should leave this place. It's sick. Oh, and Finn misses his brother. He doesn't act like it, but a girl can tell." Without waiting for him to reply, or worse, for one of them to change their minds, I walk straight on out.

***

The sun is going down as I step back out onto the street. I pause for a moment in front of the wide glass doors, looking up at the sky as it turns pink. I hadn't been so sure, when I walked in, that I'd be seeing the sky again anytime soon. But here I am. And it's time to leave town. To start something new.

In the stream of slow traffic passing by on the multi-lane road of the business district, one car comes slowly to a stop at the curb. My eyes are drawn down to it as the tinted window lowers, revealing the driver.

I grin from ear to ear, skipping around to the passenger door. Throwing myself into the seat, I pull the door closed behind me. When Finn reaches across and squeezes my thigh, I tilt my head toward him, taking in the mischievous grin on his lips.

Glancing past him at the Bici offices, I ask, "Right outside? A little risky, don't you think?"

Pulling away from the curb, he laughs. "What's life without a little risk, huh?"

"So, where to?" I ask as we melt into the traffic. "I've been advised we should both seek employment elsewhere."

Finn laughs. "Wherever you want, Elsie. I'll be right there beside you."

Epilogue

"Mmm," Finn sighs, waking up as I wriggle against him.

The sound of the ocean washes over us with the morning sun, waking me up with the immediate knowledge that I'm officially in paradise.

My leg is hitched across his hips, my face nuzzled against his neck. We arrived at the island yesterday, and it's been mostly this so far. But I have one last thing I'm still determined to achieve before our vacation ends—though when that will be, I have no plans on.

"I don't think this counts as on top," he murmurs as I take him in my hand.

I smile. "I agree completely." Then I'm scooting downwards, under the light sheet as it tangles around his legs. My lips trace a line down his abdomen as I go. I hear his breath hitch already and know he's not about to fight me on this.

He's hard and ready, pulsing up against my chest as I slide further down. "That's cheating," Finn tells me, his heart not really in the words.

"Tit for tat," I whisper as I use my hand to lift him.

I slide my tongue from his base to his tip, pulling him into my mouth at the top. Whatever his next argument was about to be dies on his tongue as he jolts and curses instead. Lowering slowly, I slide down as far as I can go, almost to gagging, then equally slowly pull back up.

Gratified by his long, heavy sigh that turns into a moan as I slide back down, sucking this time, I pick up the pace a little.

"Fucking hell..."

"Mm." I lift away. "Control yourself, darling."

"Elsie, I swear..."

I grin, straightening, using my hands to crawl back over him, straddling him. I settle down on him, his cock twitching up against my sex as I let my weight be pressure onto it. "Are you going to tell me I can't be on top now?"

Finn's hands tighten on my waist. Eyes on my bare breasts, he doesn't seem to be in a state to answer my question. I lean forward and kiss him, lifting my hips a little so I can reach and position him.

I rest back slowly, taking him as my breath catches against the feel of him, and I bite his lip. Hands on my hips, Finn pulls me sharply down, so I take all of him. Breaking off the kiss with a sharp intake of breath, I lean back onto it, grinding against him.

"Mm..." he sighs, his hands on my hips encouraging me to move, to ride.

I bite my lip and put my hands over his. "Uh-uh. Don't be impatient..." I tease, moving oh so slowly, letting the heat build.

When he looks about ready to pin me down and do it his way, I pick up the pace until I'm gyrating, riding him fast. I plant my hands on his chest, my nails digging in just slightly, bracing myself as my head tilts back and I feel my edge come to greet me.

He's nearly there too, but I let go first, relying on his hands now to guide me through my own jerkiness, as I cry out and lose myself. As my orgasm fades into a warm glow, and my limbs feel heavy, I lean down over him, letting him take the lead, hugging me down onto him as he thrusts upwards. Finn's arms tighten around me, squeezing as I feel him spend himself, as his breath jolts out in gasps.

Once he goes lax, I collapse over him, spent enough to almost fall asleep like that. "Worth the wait," I tease.

Finn laughs, making a noise that's sort of agreement. I roll off him, though my leg stays stretched across his hips, tangled in the sheet. Face turning toward me, he asks, "So, what do you want to do today? Besides that."

I sigh expansively. "Oh, you know, eat, sunbathe, shop."

"Sunbathing, huh?" He grins.

I roll my eyes. "You're insatiable." But I'm not complaining.

"Anything else?" he asks.

I sit up, gazing out at the beach. The island was a good idea, but... "Hm, I think not today or tomorrow, perhaps not even next week, we could go back to Seahorse. There's more we could do for them. And..." I add with a grin, "I wouldn't mind causing a little mischief again."

"Oh, yeah?"

"Mm-hm." I grin. "Can't have Bici forgetting us now, can we?"

Finn sits up, chin on my shoulder. His eyes sparkle. "I agree completely."

***

The End

***

Thank you so much for reading

***

Continue this series with Unlawful Entanglements, Book 2

About the author

If you liked this book, it would make my day if you'd leave a review!

***

Eva has been writing stories for as long as she can remember, simply for the joy of getting something from her imagination onto the page. Now, after many years of writing as an outlet, a hobby and especially as a necessity to staying sane, she has too many stories even for her to read.

When she isn't daydreaming while she's supposed to be doing chores, Eva loves to kayak, free-dive, swim, and in general just be near large bodies of water.

Eva's romance loves are smart and witty heroines, heroes who deserve them, minimal-to-zero OW drama, and high chemistry.

Her wish is to share her stories for others to love as well.

***

Find Eva on Facebook: Eva Heart Romance Author

***

Follow Eva on Instagram: @evaheartbook

***

View Eva's Website: Linked on Socials

***

Also by Eva

Read on for your sneak peek of Unlawful Entanglements, Book Two of the Beyond the Law Series, out 29 February

Beyond the Law Book Two

Unlawful Entanglements

Chapter One

I walk out to the kitchen with my laptop balancing on my forearm, so I can still tap through my latest job as I go. This was a good one, getting paid to 'vulnerability test,' as they call it. There's something nice about getting paid this much to effectively cause no harm. And being able to do the whole thing in my pyjamas to boot.

In my hyper-focus, as I am sometimes prone to do, I've completely skipped dinner, and now it's almost midnight and time for a snack.

I don't turn the lights on. I've been in this apartment long enough to know where everything is, and besides, the laptop screen is shining its blue-white light back at me, and it's got my full attention.

Opening the fridge, I turn so that the kitchen island and the open-plan living room beyond it are on my right.

That's when the screen, and by some degree the fridge, ceases to have my full attention.

It's something in the corner of my eye, or else some instinct pressing on my consciousness, urging me to glance up. To glance up... and see the dude on my couch.

"Jesus fucking Christ!" I gasp, my laptop going flying across the kitchen island and landing with a telling smash on the other side.

"Bridget," the man in my living room says. Not with any particular inflection. He could be greeting me from across a desk. In a building that's not my home. In the *daytime*. But he's not. He's sitting in my armchair in the dark.

Given the line of business I occasionally dabble in, which is not always so savoury as 'vulnerability testing,' I should be used to, or at least expect, people to appear after dark in my house sometimes. But I'm not used to it. Admitting the possibility, after all, is not the same thing as being faced with the reality, and I do perhaps the least useful thing, which is freeze.

What isn't helping is that the man is evidently huge. My armchair is big and soft—perfect for me to curl up in with my laptop or, occasionally, a book. But he barely fits into it, and even in the dim light as my eyes adjust, I can tell it's not a soft and slow kind of big. The kind you can sprint away from.

"What do you want?" I manage to ask, my voice shaky. My mace is in my handbag, which is hanging on the front door, which is past the giant in my living room. Not ideal.

"I'm not going to hurt you," the intruder says as he stands, which really feels like something someone who *is* going to hurt me might say.

I instinctively take a step back, and as I do, my shoulder sets my rack of hanging pots and pans jingling. In a moment of bravado, I grab one, holding it out towards him like... what? A sword? He doesn't move. I sidestep over to the light switch, still bracing the pot out in front, and flick on the light.

Then I'm frozen again, or at least my mouth is.

It can't be… But no, even these years later, the dark blonde, faintly orange hair, the green eyes… It takes me a moment, but… "*Theo*?"

"Bridget," he says evenly. It really is him. He certainly hasn't learned to use more words in the intervening time, that much is evident.

"Jesus fucking Christ," I say again, but it's more of a mutter this time. He was already big back then. But he got… well, *bigger*. He filled out, as my mother might say.

"Hi." Theo clears his throat.

"*Hi*?" I sound shrill, but I'm not about to concern myself with that. "You show up in my apartment after dumping me for law school ten years ago, and what you've got to say is *hi*?"

"I didn't *dump* you," Theo corrects with a grimace. "And it hasn't been quite ten…"

I'm still holding the pot. I forgot about that. My arm is starting to shake. I should have picked a lighter one. I drop it to my side, slicing my free hand through the air as I close my eyes and pretend this isn't happening. "You know, actually, I don't care!" I use the pot to point at the door. "*Get out*."

"I wouldn't be here if I had any choice, Bridget."

"As always, Theo, you know just what a girl wants to hear. Now…"

Before I can order him out of my apartment again, Theo says, "I need your help."

I take a long, steadying breath.

It doesn't work. I put the pot down on the kitchen island and take a moment to press my fingers to my eyes. He waits, patiently, on the other side of the counter. He always was patient; he had that going for him, at least. *Don't forget his amazing…* I silence that thought before it can conjure memories that are more sensual in nature.

I try the long breath again. Dropping my hands, I look at him properly this time. Maybe a burglar would have been preferable. The jury's out, I guess.

"In five words or less," I say, with admirable calm. "Tell me why you're here."

Theo's gaze lifts briefly skyward. Then comes back down. "I work at Bici now."

Definitely, the burglar would have been the better choice. Theo must catch something in my expression because he shifts from foot to foot, the faintest hints of humour invading his perpetually serious expression. "I'm not here to arrest you."

"*Oh*?" I clear my throat and try again, this time without making it sound like a question. "Oh..."

"Could we sit?" He tries, eyeing me like I might drop any minute.

I shake my head emphatically. "Absolutely not."

Sighing, like he expected as much, Theo steps around what remains of my laptop and leans his fists on the counter. "We know you've been working in communications and... let's call it *research*, for Seahorse. Not to mention other organisations of disrepute."

I'm hardly going to flatter myself into thinking he is just interested in what I was up to these past years. I'm a person of interest, evidently.

"Is that a question?" I ask. "Should I get a lawyer?"

"It's not a question. And you don't need a lawyer. I already said I'm not here to arrest you."

"Uh-huh..."

"You also had dealings with an organisation called Owl."

"That was a long time ago," I blurt. Like it matters what he thinks of me, or how long ago it was that I was close and personal with an assassin organisation. "Owl was, I mean. Before I found out..." I bite my tongue. *Why don't you just write out all the things he can arrest you for, idiot?*

"Before what?" Theo presses, holding my eye. "Before you knew they ran on assassinations? Did you ever find them information on a victim?"

My eyes narrow. I bristle. "I think you've exceeded your word limit to tell me what the hell you're doing in my apartment. In the middle of the night!"

Theo nods slowly, thoughtfully, reaching some conclusion I struggle to guess at. Then he straightens, and just like that, he's leaving. "Tomorrow, eleven AM, Cups and Cookie," he calls back, naming a hipster little cafe not far from here. "If you want redemption, meet me there."

Then he's gone. My apartment feels too quiet, too empty and spacious all of a sudden. And a lot less secure. I hug my arms around myself.

Only now do I remember that I'm wearing a onesie styled like a big yellow duck. I groan. *Perfect.* Just the thing anyone wants to run into their ex wearing.

No wonder he almost cracked a smile.

***

Beyond the Law Series

www.ingramcontent.com/pod-product-compliance
Lightning Source LLC
Chambersburg PA
CBHW031429150726

47989CB00002B/873